CRACKED PORCELAIN

ACTS OF ABUSE PART TWO

BROKEN WINGS AND LOST SOULS

WORKBOOK PRESS LLC
187 E Warm Springs Rd,
Suite B285, Las Vegas, NV 89119, USA

Website:	https://workbookpress.com/
Hotline:	1-888-818-4856
Email:	admin@workbookpress.com

Ordering Information:
Quantity sales. Special discounts are available on quantity purchases by corporations, associations, and others. For details, contact the publisher at the address above.

ISBN-13:	978-1-957618-19-7 (Paperback Version)
	978-1-957618-18-0 (Digital Version)

REV. DATE: 1.28.2022

S R SUTTON

CRACKED PORCELAIN

ACTS OF ABUSE PART TWO

A complete fictitious story about Ruth Ashley and her life as a nurse and model following her harrowing life and looking in to her past experiences of abuse. This story shows highlights the many emotions and nightmares as well as other effects following experiences of abuse. It also deals with lesbian relationships and societies reactions to same sex relationships, as Ruth discovers her own sexuality amidst the chaos and animosity around her. Some people may find this book disturbing particularly if you have experienced abuse of any kind, whether it be physical, mental, psychological or financial. You are advised to seek help if this is the case you can find useful websites at the end of the book.

DEDICATIONS

This book is dedicated to people who have made a difference to our society, the voices of the people who are not afraid to speak out and be noticed. I speak of many people who have even given their live for a cause because their voice matters. I speak of people who speak out about the oppression and the abuse, as well as those who fight for the weak and encourage the strong to be with them. People like Martin Luther King, Nelson Mandela, John and Yoko who have made their feelings known about peace and to Emma Watson for her remarkable speech on sexual equality. For the gay pride that makes a difference to the gay population and their freedom, Manchester pride has an impact on the city (Don't forget the festival every August). I could name many more like the many crises teams, some of which are featured on the back of the book. I also refer to the mental health teams all over the world who have a difficult task in helping those less fortunate than ourselves, may they be rewarded for their efforts.

ACKNOWLEDGEMENTS

TO MY PARENTS RITA AND LEN
SUTTON R.I.P

Thank you as usual to all my family and friends for your support in my endeavor to get my message across, I speak of hope, freedom gender equality and fighting against all kinds of abuse. Thank you Gemma, Jeni, Mike and Dan may you all reach your ultimate goals in life and whatever you do I am proud of you all. A special thanks to Rachel Day for her editing work and interest in my projects and thank you to my friends and colleagues for their support unfortunately I am not able to mention them all.

CRACKED PORCELAIN
ACTS OF ABUSE PART TWO
BROKEN WINGS AND LOST SOULS

KILLER QUEEN

A young man stands posing naked in front of a full length mirror; he wore a wig and make up. he has one of his favourite Queen songs on his C.D player called 'Bohemian rhapsody' and he is miming to the song and practicing dance moves almost like a ballerina. He is room appears tidy for a man, and displayed posters of Freddie Mercury everywhere. He was evidently a fan of Queen by the amount of songs he was playing and by the way he mimicked Freddie Mercury's moves, as he would have performed them on stage. But this young man appeared to perform in a more feminine way as if he had been observing a young woman's movements, he used his arms and legs like a mime artist and his body seemed to float on air. He was a slim youth in his mid twenties who was dancing to Queen he had short brown hair, large brown eyes with a rather unusually soft smooth complexion. Apart from his posters of Freddie Mercury, Colin had photographs of Ruth Ashley when she was modelling with Pamela, she seemed to catch his eye and he blew kisses to her while he was dancing.

It was a summers evening in the early part of the week, the streets were quiet and only a few people were roaming about. Amongst these people was Ruth a slim woman with long dark flowing hair and large brown eyes. Ruth had a look of melancholy, that some would mistake for sadness. Although she would have every reason to be sad, judging by her tragic past, living with a psychopath called Malcolm who murdered her mother and her girlfriend amongst others. Ruth is a mental health nurse who worked in the local hospital acute mental health unit, dealing with all kind of conditions from by polar, schizophrenia and clinical depression. Ruth had been deep in thought when she was suddenly distracted by a speeding car passing by playing loud music. She jumped and then returned to her thoughts unaware that someone was following her. It was a slim youth with short brown hair, large brown eyes and a rather unusually soft smooth complexion and a feminine walk, He had headphones on playing his favourite music by the group 'Queen'. Ruth entered a bar and joined a few friends after a few seconds she walked the bar with one of her friends and ordered drinks. The youth stood at the bar, removed his headphones and stood close enough to hear their conversation, but remaining silent. Ruth was discussing relationships making it known about her sexuality by her choice of words and from her tone of voice.

"Look Kathy, I don't care what people say at work they all know that I am a lesbian, why should I hide it the whole world knows after my appearance on TV and radio as well as the press" Ruth said

"Ruth that was when you were in modelling now you're back

in nursing and all that's behind you" Kathy said concerned.

"I might have stopped modelling but I haven't stopped being a lesbian, that's me and my sexuality" Ruth said trying to explain to her friend.

Kathy was a blonde woman with shorter hair and built slightly larger than Ruth, she was listening intently to Ruth along with the youth who by now had bought himself a drink. He kept glancing at Ruth's beautiful face watching her mannerisms then making similar movements as if he was deliberately copying her. But was this young man a stalker or had he got a more sinister thought in mind, he had sat down and made a point of staring at her, if Ruth had not been so busy maybe she would have noticed him watching her and feel uneasy. But Ruth was too occupied and engrossed in her own thoughts and conversation to be bothered with anyone else. After a while the young man left the bar and headed down the street, but he continued to mimic Ruth's movements and when he arrived home he practiced them in a mirror. Talking with his mouth and hands as Ruth did, even giving a smile as if to express empathy and then look away as if to get distracted. Usually she would then play with her hair and tighten her lips with a reluctance to continue speaking, allowing others to have their say. Ruth was very expressive with her eye, mouth and the way she held her head, so many things to copy but the young man seemed to master it all.

The next morning Ruth picked Kathy up for work, she was sat in the car looking in front of her at a busy street. She was relieved that she was not in the crowd as she particularly hated crowds of people and the closeness of strangers. She felt intimidated and very vulnerable when people brushed passed her especially men, fat men with horrible sweaty bodies and eyes that undressed her. She felt secure in her car almost as comfortable as being in her wardrobe, that dark and solitary place that she was safe in, as long as she remained silent.

Kathy made her jump as she suddenly opened the door and shouted "Good morning" She was so bubbly and bright where Ruth took a long time to revive from her slumber and confessed to being grumpy.

"Did I startle you sorry Ruth" Kathy said sorting out her bags.

"It's okay Kathy I was deep in thought" Ruth said smiling.

"You're worried I can tell, what's troubling you?" Kathy asked concerned.

"The usual thoughts I suppose and nightmares" Ruth replied.

"Come on Ruth we discussed this, you must think positive and believe in yourself". Kathy insisted.

"I know your right I hear your voice in my thoughts and try to be positive" Ruth began to drive away.

"I read something that you wrote about some time ago saying, if you visit your saddest place you will find me there, amidst the broken wings and lost souls. Hold back your tears for your memories lie like peaceful doves in a tree, so peaceful, so white and pure. Remember those broken wings and lost souls, those forgotten dreams and ambitions that once captivated your heart, yet a glimmer of hope, flicker of light appears in the darkness taking you into the light, far from the dark and solitary place. New hopes, new dreams and a bright future await me, my positive thoughts and warm heart goes forth into the light." Kathy read the words from a sheet of paper.

"My words and you kept them" Ruth said holding back the tears.

"Yes to remind me that you can think positive, I will quote these words whenever you're negative" Kathy said firmly.

"Thank you Kathy" Ruth replied

"Don't mention it" Kathy said dismissively.

They arrived at the hospital and parked the car near a wall; Kathy was the first to step out of the car followed by Ruth who swept her hair back from her face with her hands. Kathy laughed as the wind blew it back into her face, she laughed because her hair was fairly short and more manageable. Close by the young man continued to watch Ruth and was also amused by Ruth's actions, trying to mimic her while playing his favourite Queen music 'you're my best friend'. He watched them enter the building on the mental health unit; he seemed to wait for a while in the car park before entering into another building.

He had entered accident and emergency and wandered into the toilets, he sat in a cubical and proceeded to expose his arms, he was a thin man who looked effeminate and timid. He produced a knife from his shoulder bag and held the blade against his wrist, with a deep breath he cut across his wrist one and then again until he began to bleed onto the floor. He sighed with relief and watched the blood trickle onto the floor. Shortly after a pool of blood surrounded his feet and drifted under the cubical door. He heard a door shut and two people were talking, female voices he had entered the women's toilet. Suddenly one of them screamed having seen the blood, the other woman shouted out.

"Hello can you hear me, are you alright" She said.

"She could be dead" The other person said expecting a woman to be in the cubical.

"Lets get help quickly" One woman said to the other.

They sound appeared very young and inexperienced as they rushed out and ran to the receptionist. The receptionist quickly calmed them down and alerted security who ran into the toilet to deal with the situation followed by a nurse. One of the security guards pushed open the door and escorted the young man to an available cubical in casualty. The nurse dealt with his wounds after a doctor was satisfied they were superficial cuts, she asked him questions about how he was feeling and soon discovered that he was suffering from clinical depression.

"So what's your name?" The nurse asked.

"Colin" He replied.

"My names Kim" she said washing his arm "So Colin why do this?"

"I wanted to end it all, nothing to live for" Colin said in pain.

"So how long have you felt this way?" Kim asked.

"A while now ever since my parents were killed in a car accident" Colin said avoiding eye contact.

"Sorry to hear that Colin, I will get some help for you,

maybe you can discuss this with a psychiatric nurse" Kim said bandaging his arm.

"Okay" Colin agreed.

After a discussion with the psychiatric liaison nurse Colin agreed to be admitted onto the mental health unit for assessment. Colin seemed pleased to be there and even more so when he saw Ruth walking down the corridor towards him.

"Hello Colin I am Ruth" She said smiling "Come with me and we can talk about your stay".

Colin sat in a room with Ruth spending most of the time watching her mannerisms, he was interested in her eye movements and the way she used her hands to express herself. She spoke with her hands her fingers seemed to move about like a musical conductor and she seemed to touch her hair a lot. She seemed aggravated by her hair being tied back in a bobble and seemed to fidget constantly as if she was uneasy being sat down.

"I like your eyes" Colin said staring at her large brown eyes.

"Thank you" Ruth replied trying to concentrate on the interview.

"You have long shiny hair and lovely teeth" He continued

"Can we just stay focused on the interview please Colin" Ruth said feeling very uncomfortable.

"I am sorry I didn't mean to embarrass you" He said looking away.

"Colin where are your parents?" Ruth asked

"They are dead, killed in a car crash" Colin said looking out of the window onto the ward.

"Colin that's not true is it?" Ruth said sternly.

"Yes they got crushed in the seats like melons" He insisted.

"No they are alive and well, I spoke to them earlier" Ruth watched Colin's eye movements which told her he was avoiding the truth.

"Why are you lying to me Colin?" She asked trying to get his attention "Are you upset with me because I stopped you talking about me?"

"No I just hate them; I can't help saying things about you because you are beautiful" Colin admitted.

"I am flattered but I need to be professional and you are a patient" Ruth said trying to explain the rules about patient and staff involvements.

"I don't fancy you, it's not like that and I know that you are a lesbian" Colin said in a bluntly.

"Well, that's my personal choice and my life Colin" Ruth said defensively.

"I am sorry really but I am really not happy and I want to change my life even my parents" Colin said coldly.

Ruth felt a shiver running down her spine as Colin related his feelings about his parents and his school life, He spoke about everyone having no eyes and of how he had nightmares of blinding everyone so that only he could see. He discussed many things but nothing positive as if he could only see the bad in everyone, all except Ruth who he admired.

Ruth finished the interview feeling mentally drained, she was tired and even her speech was slurred when she was relaying the entire conversation to Kathy.

"Colin is clearly besotted with you" Kathy said smiling.

"Oh come on Kathy he's a boy and living in a fantasy world" Ruth said unconvinced by his explanations.

"Ruth I am joking he is psychotic and has a warped mind, he is unhappy and relates to you for some reason" Kathy appeared satisfied that Colin was just depressed and lonely.

"So I can relax then and not worry about another possible psychopath?" Ruth said with a sigh.

"He appears to have a psychosis but I wouldn't worry about anything your safe" Kathy reassured Ruth.

The following day Ruth was back on the ward going about her duties as a nurse, the usual activities took place such as handover from the night staff to day staff reporting on each patient in turn including Colin. No problems were reported, no violence or suicides nothing to really say of significance, a quick handover and the night staff went home while the day staff took over the care. But throughout Ruth's twelve-hour shift Colin had been watching her every time she was in view either on the ward or in the office. He studied every movement from her walk, gestures and posture; he listened to her speaking and instructing the staff to carry out duties. He continued to do every shift that she was on, she was oblivious to this and hardly ever came in contact with him until one day. Ruth was passing his room and overheard him talking to himself and looking in the mirror, behaving just like her, every movement was exactly like hers.

"Now listen to me you know what to do so carry on all of you" Colin said.

Ruth went cold hearing and eventually seeing him impersonating her and when Kathy came on duty she explained everything to her.

"Ruth are you sure about this, or is it about the other day when he appeared to fancy you?" Kathy said in disbelief.

"For fuck sake Kathy he is freaking me out" Ruth said angrily.

"Calm down Ruth he is harmless, don't go by past experiences your becoming paranoid" Kathy said trying to reassure Ruth that Colin's actions were normal.

"He is probably tormenting you or teasing you and your letting him get to you" Kathy explained "He's a healthy teenager who has a crush on you".

"I wish he would have a fucking crush on someone else, like you or one of the other staff" Ruth said looking out of the office window onto the ward.

"You ought to feel flattered not insulted" Kathy said watching him walking down the corridor.

"I just feel as if there is something else about him that we haven't seen yet" Ruth said watching him look at her from a distance.

"Oh once again paranoia, I really don't agree Ruth" Kathy dismissed Ruth's claim and started writing notes.

A month passed by and Colin had been treated with medication and a course of electric convulsive treatment (E.C.T) He left the hospital on Fluoxetine (Prozac) He appeared more positive and able to cope with life a little better or so the experts were led to believe, Ruth reserved judgement and felt a little easier when he had finally left the hospital. She felt his eyes on her each time she was on duty and she couldn't relax at anytime at work, even her home life was affected when Cheryl was out visiting family Ruth stayed home and found she had to go out to a bar with Sheena and Gloria or Kathy at times to prevent being alone. She had a feeling something was going to happen at some point and craved company; this was not like Ruth not even when she was being pursued by Malcolm years before.

In the meantime, Colin was in his apartment looking in the mirror, he began talking to his reflection.

"Oh Ruth you don't know how alike we are; don't worry I will protect you from harm my darling" Colin leaned forward in the mirror "But I am Ruth I will protect me".

Colin began to act just like Ruth he started fidgeting and mimicking all the movement that he had observed on the ward, he stood up and walked like her across the room. He had studied her make up from seeing her out at night in local bars; this led to him putting on make up and continuing to talk like her. He had returned to the mirror continuing to speak, his voice sounded eerie and then he put on a dark wig resembling her hair.

"Perfect" He said playing with it with his hands just like Ruth does.

He had photos of her from her modelling days all around the mirror, each photograph had been chosen showing her flowing hair and soft silky complexion. Unblemished looks that were specially designed to appear good by photographers, Ruth used to marvel at how they made her seem so flawless. Ruth considered herself like Pamela her dead girl friend and sister, when she was modelling 'cracked porcelain' attractive on the outside yet scarred on the inside due to past abuse. But Colin was unaware of her abuse or most of her past, although he read about Malcolm and Frank in 'Criminal world' magazine.

Colin sat for hours in front of the mirror and continued speaking and mimicking Ruth, he was having a complete conversation with himself as Colin then as Ruth.

"Kathy who gives a fuck that I am a lesbian its my life and I will live it how I choose, no one should be harmed for their choice in gender and what's more any fucker who does try to harm them I will deal with them".

"But Ruth you will get in trouble" Colin responded to his female voice.

"Not me I will be discrete, I will pursue them in darkness and kill them quietly" He replied as Ruth producing a knife from a handbag "Cut and tear without a care, half a pound of two penny rice, half a pound of treacle this is the way I cut with a knife, I bleed you like treacle".

Colin prepared his outfit dressing like Ruth in a pair of dark jeans and a white blouse then put on a small black leather jacket. Then he walked towards the door and opened it placing the handbag neatly over his shoulder before leaving the apartment. His last words before leaving was "Dressed to kill" how ironic were those words as he set out to pursue a woman who had argued with Ruth a few weeks before, she spoke against Lesbianism.

Colin walked for a while before seeing the woman in question, he waited for the opportune moment and when she was alone in a dark alley, he stopped her and spoke like Ruth.

"Do you know who I am?" He asked

"Ruth the gay woman" She replied

"Oh very good" He said sarcastically "So you don't like gays?"

"Wait are you trying to pick a fight, are you drunk?" She asked

"Fuck you bitch I am sober, but I don't like you" He continued

"Look I am not against gays each to their own as long as you don't bother me" She sounded nervous and began walking backwards against a wall.

"You fucking liar I know what you really think" He began fidgeting and pulled a knife from the handbag.

"I told you I don't want trouble; I just want to go home" She said in a quivering voice

Colin put the knife to her throat and forced the blade across her neck cutting her deeply and then stabbed her in the abdomen. She dropped to the ground landing at his feet; he could feel her body still moving for a while then nothing. After a short while he walked calmly away as if nothing had happened, he seemed to make it obvious that people saw him walking down the street deliberately bumping into people.

The following day the murder was on the news and in the papers causing a lot of people to discuss the incident. Ruth was going to work it was Kathy's turn to pick Ruth up from her apartment. Ruth was late and looked particularly tired as she entered Kathy's car, she slumped into the seat wearing dark jeans and a white blouse with a spec of blood on the sleeve. Kathy didn't notice it as it was on the opposite side to where she was sitting in the passenger seat.

"Morning Ruth did you have a rough night?" Kathy asked looking at her tired eyes.

"Oh yes how did you know?" Ruth asked

"Well you look awful" Kathy said honestly

"Oh thanks Kathy that what a lady wants to hear in the morning" Ruth said feeling hurt.

"You a lady don't make me laugh" Kathy replied laughing

"Well shit to you Kathy dear" Ruth said almost smiling

"You see that's what I mean" Kathy continued "The gob on you"

"You wouldn't have me any different" Ruth said smiling.

"Well at least I got you smiling" Kathy said driving along to the hospital

When they arrived Kathy mentioned the murder and hoped

that Ruth had seen the news too, but Ruth hardly ever switched the television on in the morning. She never even had the radio on that morning.

"I just caught a glimpse of the new this morning Ruth so I just heard it was a murder near you, down some alley". Kathy explained

"I haven't heard anything" Ruth replied "A bit scary though".

As Ruth stepped out of the car Kathy noticed the blood on her sleeve, she couldn't take her eyes off it and made it obvious to Ruth that she had seen it.

"What have you done Ruth?" Kathy asked

"Oh shit I must have caught my arm on some broken glass" Ruth said hesitantly.

"So when did you do that?" Kathy asked concerned.

"I don't know" Ruth replied abruptly "I am okay"

They entered the hospital finding that everybody was discussing the murder; Ruth was surprised by the presence of police who were questioning people in the area. She was surprised as two officers approached her one of them grabbed her arm and noticed the blood, without hesitation he arrested her and they led her to a police car.

"What the fucks going on?" Ruth shouted

"Your under arrest" One of the officers said

"What on earth for?" Ruth yelled

"Just come quietly" Said the other policeman

When they arrived at the police station Ruth was taken downstairs and locked in a police cell, she remained there while the police pieced together evidence enough to officially arrest her. Ruth sat thinking about previous events, she realised that the blood on her blouse was from her leg. She had scratched it badly in the night self harming from night terrors, but the police wouldn't believe this. She needed either Kathy or her girl friend Cheryl to be there in order to confirm her story, although even Kathy suspected that she was somehow involved in the murder.

After a while Ruth heard someone at the cell door and the sound of keys unlocking it. Two officers stood outside and eventually entered the room; they led Ruth out of the cell, up the stairs and into a small room with a table and four chairs. To her surprise Kathy was sat in one of the chairs, she gave a sigh of relief and greeted her warmly with a hug.

"Kathy what's happening?" Ruth said desperately.

"You are being questioned for that girl's murder" Kathy replied "But don't worry I know your innocent".

The police officers sat opposite, the one introduced himself, he was a large fat man with odd teeth and bad breath.

"My name is detective George Mills and this is my colleague Gary" He said introducing his colleague who was a little smaller than him and had a kinder face.

"Gary switched on the tape while George quoted the date, time and details of the suspect and introduction to interview. George also had a package in his hand and seemed to be clutching it as if it was going to escape, he also had a smug look on his face as he proceeded to interview Ruth.

"Now we could make this as easy or as hard as you like Ruth" George began "I mean if you cooperate we can be finished and the job will be easy".

"Where were you last night?" George asked

"I was at home for a while and then I went for a walk to Sankey's bar" Ruth said calmly.

"Did anybody see you there?" Gary asked "it's a big place but nice"

"Yes it is nice and I was there with my friends Gloria and Sheena".

"What time did you leave?" George asked

"About 11pm I needed to get home in order to go bed, as I was up early for work" Ruth said looking at George then Gary.

"We need you to go with a female officer and get changed out of those clothes, we need to examine them" George said

"What's going on am I being accused of murder? Ruth asked

"Ruth just cooperate please" Kathy pleaded

Ruth stood up and took some clothes from Kathy, she then left the room with a female officer. Soon after she returned dressed in some of her other clothes, she seemed less relaxed and less willing to cooperate.

Gary switched on the tape and the interview resumed Ruth tried not to give George eye contact as he resembled her father's friend and her abuser.

"So would you mind telling me where you got the blood on the blouse?" George asked

"It's from my leg I scratched them in the night" Ruth explained

"Oh, you mean when you were struggling with Janet?" George asked

"Janet?" Ruth asked puzzled.

"The woman you murdered" George said

"I didn't murder anyone" Ruth said shaking

"Oh you mean it was an accident" George continued

"No I mean I never met her or had anything to do with her" Ruth said looking at Kathy

"Well we have witnesses who say you had an argument with her months ago in non other than Sankey's bar" George sat back and again seemed to have a smug expression on his face.

"I remember an argument with a woman who insulted me, she was with a group of women who had been drinking" Ruth recollected.

Gary edged forward and looked into Ruth's large brown eyes, he was watching her expressions and eye movements as George was questioning her.

"I can understand you feeling angry and upset, possibly humiliated by what she said, maybe you had good cause to fight with her. But then it got out of hand and you killed her, no one would blame you for getting upset. What did she say to you?" Gary asked

"She was going on about my sexuality, saying that I was a lesbian who flaunted my sexuality on TV as a model with my friend Pamela" Ruth explained

"What a waste you're so beautiful, so I bet you were angry" Gary said trying to extract more information out of her.

"Thank you and yes I was fucking angry" Ruth replied

Kathy touch her hand and looked at her as if to say stay calm, but she felt her sweaty palm and her fingers were shaking.

"Is Kathy your girl friend Ruth?" George asked watching Kathy trying to comfort her.

"No, she's my friend my girl friend is Cheryl she is probably waiting for me outside this room" Ruth said glancing at George.

"Why can't you look at me when I am talking to you Ruth, is it guilt?" George baited her.

"No not at all I find you repulsive and fucking rude as shit" Ruth said almost spitting in his face.

At that moment she proceeded to vomit, Kathy grabbed a rubbish bin and tissues from the desk. Ruth continued to retch and brought up copious amounts of fluid that made Gary move away from the table.

"This is normal for Ruth" Kathy said rubbing her back

"I'm okay" Ruth said "Sorry Kathy"

"Shall we continue?" George asked

"Why not go for it big boy" Ruth said "Do your worst you obviously think I am guilty".

"Are you okay Ruth" Gary asked

"Oh are you playing good cop bad cop very cute" Ruth said with tears forming in her eyes "You are fucking pathetic honestly, one who acts like a prick and the other complements me"

"We need to show you a tape from CT footage see what you think" George said putting a video into a player.

The video showed a figure walking down a street near the crime scene; the person was walking along with a hand bag over the left shoulder and touching her face with her left hand. It was dark and the street was dimly lit with a few street lamps, she stopped for a while looked around and then continued.

"This is you isn't it?" George asked

"No certainly not" Ruth replied "But it looks like me I must admit".

"It is you I am sure of it and so were witnesses who saw you out that night" George said

"I haven't got a handbag like that" Ruth said noticing the white handbag

"And if you look carefully that person is carrying it over her left shoulder, and using her left hand to do things". Kathy said pointing.

"So what does that mean?" George asked in a highly

intellectual manner.

"George the person on the video is left handed, he is also a male" Gary pointed out to George's disappointment.

"It is not apparent from the outset but watch his walk and the general mannerisms" Kathy said as George reversed and reran the tape.

"Colin" Ruth said "It has to be Colin"

"Ruth that's ridiculous" Kathy said dismissively.

At that moment a knock came at the door, almost immediately afterwards the police woman enters the room. She took George to one side and he seemed to get annoyed by what she said to him.

"Well it seems your innocent and I must apologise" George obviously wasn't used to apologising and being humble, however he was presented with evidence showing that she was innocent.

"I would however appreciate your help with my enquiries as you seemed to know Colin Bailey" George said trying not to look at Ruth

"How does fuck off sound" Ruth said angrily.

"Ruth we have to help" Kathy said abruptly.

"Why the hell should I help them with what they put me through" Ruth said frowning at George

"Because you're the stronger person and we must stop" Kathy paused for a moment "Wait a minute we never mentioned Colin's surname".

"Oh he rang asking what was happening to Ruth, when you mentioned Colin we realised who he was" George explained

"So you were right about Colin" Kathy said to Ruth "I am sorry for doubting you and I should have listened to you in view of past events".

Kathy also realised why Ruth vomited and walked over to George, she looked him up and down then stared into his eyes.

"Ruth is right you are a creep" Kathy winked at Ruth then sat her down.

They both explained about Colin and the way he behaved, discussing about him being obsessed with Ruth and copying her mannerisms. It was obvious by now that Colin in his own mind wanted to become Ruth and modelled himself off like her, he even dressed like her. But what was worse he killed the people who were likely to harm her; Janet was only one of many victims discovered while Ruth was in the police cell. A total of five bodies were discovered in various locations around Manchester and the greater Manchester area, Colin dressed as Ruth and went on a spree of murders trying to justify his actions by saying Ruth was defending herself. But who really knows what is in the mind of a killer, he was not sexually attracted to her, neither was a homosexual or transsexual in the true sense of the word. Ruth could except any type of sexual preference and mixed with all genders, frequenting the gay village for fun. She was in a lesbian relationship with Cheryl but failed to understand Colin who dressed like her and killed people because they offended Ruth. What was worse Colin remained on the streets and could attack someone else at any time, only Ruth could stop him killing again or could she?

Colin used music to help motivate himself to go out and kill more women, it always seemed to be songs by the pop group queen. 'Another one bites the dust' and 'Don't stop me now' was his favourite songs, although 'We will rock you' was the one he played most and killer queen as his second choice. He was speeding in his car when he used to play 'don't stop me now'.

The police raided Colin's apartment and discovered all the photographs of Ruth and then found photographs of Colin dressed like Ruth, it was clearly evident that Colin was the murderer posing as Ruth. Much as Colin tried to simulate Ruth he still couldn't fully disguise himself as a female, it was sad but he really wanted to be Ruth for some reason. With this in mind he was still on the streets somewhere and even though Ruth felt safe, he was unpredictable.

Ruth was being watched by the police as she tried to lead a normal life, they knew that he would have to contact her at some stage, either at her apartment, at Emma's house were her step mother Diane once lived or at one of the bars that Ruth frequented. Ruth just had to be herself and wait for Colin to contact her, she was like bait on a hook trying to catch a fish. She was moving about for weeks before something happened, then the moment she was actually alone in a toilet cubical in one of the night clubs Colin appeared dressed like Ruth.

"I have missed you Ruth, have you been avoiding me" Colin said locking the toilet door.

"Colin, where have you been?" Ruth said nervously

"Oh you know here and there" Colin replied "And call me Ruth after all I am you now, I killed as Ruth and now I have become you".

"I don't understand" Ruth replied

"Well there is no room for both of us and so one of us must die" Colin produced the knife from his white handbag.

"You know the police are aware that you murdered those women, how many did you kill, four or five?" Ruth asked glancing at the door then back at him.

"Well six now" Colin said coldly "But that doesn't matter it's just a numbers game"

"Do you intend to kill me?" Ruth asked

There was a silence while Colin looked into a mirror "Uncanny isn't it, how much alike we are I practiced being you for months and even on the ward when they gave me that electric shock treatment I suffered to be like you"

Colin noticed her edging towards the door and jumped in her way, he held the knife to her throat and let the blade touch her flesh.

"One cut will end it all" He said then began to grin "Oh Ruth with so much beauty, so much love and compassion, a beacon of hope shining in the darkness lighting the way for so many".

"But why be like me, what have I got that you want?" Ruth asked trying not to show her fear.

"Don't make me angry or I will cut you like the others" Colin shouted "You who has beauty, love and not afraid to express yourself, you who are a lesbian but fights for your gender, you ask why be like you when you are a living legend" He said holding out his hand and slicing open the palm of his right hand. "This is your blood not mine share it with me" He said wiping it across her face then onto her right shoulder.

At that moment the door handle started to move, then came a male voice

"Ruth it's the police were coming in" The voice was that of the policeman George.

The next thing they heard was the door being rammed open by some heavy object, it took a few hard bangs before the door burst open and the police came rushing in. Colin had run towards the door and stabbed George, then he stabbed himself making sure he struck himself deeply enough to cause a fatal wound. He fell to the ground and Ruth ran over to him. She knelt down beside him and bent her head towards his mouth listening to his final words. Her eyes widened as she managed to catch his words and then take his final breath.

"There is only one Ruth and she is you" Colin said before his death.

Kathy was standing close by with Cheryl and other friends each looking at Ruth only Kathy moved forward to comfort Ruth, then Cheryl took over and led Ruth out of the nightclub. All the emergency crew were outside Ruth was helped into an ambulance with Cheryl while the others stood and watched them leave.

Amazingly Ruth did attend Colin's funeral, he was cremated

and at the ceremony the family played a song that Colin always wanted for his funeral service called ironically 'Who wants to live forever' by Queen Ruth soon recovered and she was asked to get involved in the Manchester pride festival scheduled for the end of August, by that time she would probably feel better and able to cope with one of her worst fears, which is crowded places. The festival was a busy place and Ruth was used to the gay village as Cheryl and her frequented bars there. Ruth enjoyed dressing up and she would be in familiar company and amongst friends, she loved the parade and interacting with everyone there. Of course gay pride is world wide and both her sister and she were in the New York festival last year. But the biggest problem Ruth had to face was her frequent nightmares, if only she could master them then she could live a relatively normal life. Ruth put the radio on and the Queen song played as Ruth lay down and closed her eyes 'The show must go on' how very apt.

NIGHTMARES

Reflective thoughts from Ruth's past made her have nightmares and the night terrors plagued her on occasions, Ruth had quite a past and even her present life seemed troubled with so many things happening. Cheryl often comforted her at home and Kathy was her rock at work, she reflected on her relationship with Malcolm, then his brother Frank who pursued her. Raven caused her grief and then Colin appeared dressed like her mimicking her every move, murdering women. Any other woman would have had a nervous break down or committed suicide due to all her grief but she became ever stronger and continued to help mend the broken wings and find lost souls of her patients.

Ruth had the most weird dreams probably due to her past and ward experience, sometimes wished that she had remained a model like Gloria and Sheena. Sheena Brown tried to persuade her to return to modelling and managed to get her on a few photo shoots with her. Sheena was stunning with her ginger hair and blue eyes and was so fit and healthy; she went to the gym and often went jogging with Ruth in the park. She took a good diet and drank vegetable smoothies, her skin was soft and smooth and her blue eyes sparkled. She didn't like Ruth at first, she saw her as the lesbian who stole the stage due to her sexuality, but warmed to her when she got to know the real Ruth. Ruth often rubbed people up the wrong way because of her forthright attitude that she adopted in order to survive, she managed to turn heads when she entered a room. Some would say here is Ruth the nightmare, while others would say thank god Ruth's here to fight in our corner. So was she the coolest chick in town or was she queen bitch, when anyone saw her on a poster or in the flesh they would see a mild and gentle lady, sweet and kind. Colin summed her up when he spent his last moments with her 'you have beauty, love and are not afraid to express yourself' he paid her the biggest compliment to want to actually be her.

One night Ruth fell asleep; she had been on a new course of medication called amitriptyline as an antidepressant drug taken at night. But she was suffering from some of the side effects such as visual hallucinations, confusion and vomiting. But this night she began to dream and as usual she they were quite vivid. If you could make a recipe for her nightmares it would contain half a dozen sculls, an old fat pervert and psychopath, a frightened girl hiding in a wardrobe and definitely people wearing porcelain masks. But this night she was dreaming about her sister Claire and them growing up together unaware that both of them were being abused by their father's friend who they called uncle. Who would ever know how they both suffered and for how long as it was never discussed, both kept their living nightmare secret for whatever reason they had. The truth was they were scarred forever living the nightmare both day and night, there was no escape, no comfort or reassurance that it would not occur again.

Ruth dreamt of a countryside like Pamela and her visited once miles from anywhere, Claire was with her and they had a picnic with sandwiches and fruit, they were laughing and joking feeling happy. Then came the rain and so they packed up to leave, putting everything in the boot of the car. They arrived at an old cottage near a wood, it seemed a little spooky but they needed a place to stay. Ruth knocked on the door of the cottage and waited, she was greeted by an old woman who smiled and let them in. Ruth entered first and noticed a lot of portrait paintings of men and women looking very serious, she was attracted to one painting that looked like her mother Sarah.

"Would you like a cup of tea dear?" The old lady asked

"Yes please" Ruth said feeling comfortable snuggled with her sister by the open fire.

All seemed well as the old lady returned with a tray of tea and biscuits, the tea was served in china cups and biscuits on a plate designed so neatly with a paper sheet beneath them.

"Where are you from?" She asked

"Manchester" Ruth replied

"Help yourself to biscuits" She said pointing to the neatly arranged pile on the plate "My name is Lillian"

"I am Ruth Ashley and this is my sister Claire" Ruth tapped Claire as she introduced her to Lillian.

"She looks tired your welcome to stay here overnight there is plenty of room" Lillian offered.

"Oh its fine we will be going home soon" Ruth replied eager to go.

Claire sipped her tea and nibbled onto her biscuit, Ruth was too busy looking around the room to drink. Where did you get that painting Ruth said pointing to the one that looked like her mother Sarah, it seemed so alive as the eyes followed her round the room.

"I painted that, look at the name Lillian Shaw" Lillian said

"My god you are really good" Ruth said walking up and down the room.

"The picture is simply called 'Sarah' from a live model" she informed Ruth

"Sarah, you mean you knew Sarah" Ruth said astonished

"Yes of course did you know her?" Lillian said in surprise

"Yes she was my mother" Ruth said confused

"A nice lady but she only ever mentioned Pamela to me" Lillian said staring at Ruth "So where did you come from?"

"I was from a different Father and thus adopted out to my step mother Diane" Ruth explained "I never met my real mother Sarah".

Ruth walked to the window and looked out, it was pouring down with rain and getting dark, Claire had fallen asleep and Ruth was getting tired.

"Can I take up your offer of a bed" Ruth asked

"Of course" Lillian replied

Ruth woke Claire and they went up to one of the spare rooms, it had two single beds in the room and a dressing table. Claire flopped onto the bed like a rag doll while

Ruth rested on the other bed, but remained awake for a while thinking. The next part of Ruth's dream seemed to change from pleasant to unpleasant as she heard a noise downstairs and went to investigate. Slowly she wandered down the stairs into darkness feeling the cold wooden steps to the bottom; she began feeling for the light switch but couldn't find it. Suddenly she was startled by a loud bang and a woman's voice calling out repeatedly "Sarah". Then she felt the shape of skulls around the floor and a light appeared from the distance, it all looked too familiar as they increased in numbers. Then Lillian appeared in the light and suddenly peeled the flesh off her face revealing Colin who was brandishing a sharp knife. She ran away from him and collided with another man wearing a porcelain mask which had been damaged, she pulled off his mask and Malcolm was looking at her holding a baseball bat. Another man appeared in a mask sitting in a wheelchair, he stood up and walked towards her calling Raven to come and kill her. She ran back upstairs to rescue Claire from her sleep but she was gone, leaving a trail of blood behind her for Ruth to follow. Ruth came to a wardrobe that looked familiar, it belonged to her and the room was similar to her own room. She opened the wardrobe door and Pamela appeared.

"Ruth don't be afraid we will conquer these wicked people" She said

"But you are dead?" Ruth hastily replied.

"Dead, no your mistaken I am alive" Pamela replied

But as Ruth tried to embrace her she crumbled away into dust, Ruth entered the wardrobe for safety and sat waiting for a while. Then she heard a loud noise and the wardrobe began to move it rocked and shuck until the sides disintegrated and front drifted into a light. All the faces of her past appeared all those that hated her coming closer to her in a threatening manner, the ghosts that were haunting her. She pushed her way through them feeling them trying to pull her back, but she used all her strength to escape, they also had sharp nails which scratched her arms and legs while she fled. Then she raced down the stairs finding her way to the front door, but as she opened it another door appeared. Finally, she broke free and opened the car boot, lying inside was Claire's body, covered in blood and scratch marks, her eyes staring upwards and her mouth open as if she had been startled to death. She turned to see the ghosts behind her and screamed, she eventually stopping hearing a familiar voice calling her.

"Ruth, wake up Ruth your dreaming" Cheryl said shaking her

"I was having another nightmare wasn't I?" Ruth said

"You need help Ruth, its becoming too much it can't be good for you to keep having nightmares, what would you say if one of your patients suffered like this?" Cheryl said concerned

"One of them does she even suffers by day tormented screaming and shouting, she grabs you but cannot communicate so she speaks with her hands" Ruth explained "She suffers from korsacoff syndrome due to excessive alcohol consumption".

"That must be awful, how do you manage her condition?" Cheryl asked

"It's difficult but we use medication, various techniques and divertive therapy" Ruth said "Sometimes it works she can be so relaxed, I can calm her down sometimes when she is in an elevated state".

"Ruth why don't you do some other job if it effects you like this, self harming, trashing about and injuring yourself, suffering from night terrors?" Cheryl was concerned, not just for Ruth, but also for herself as she was sleeping with her.

"I have had counselling but some of them are fucking useless, how does that make you feel, that is a common phrase that most counsellors would use, I feel like saying how the fuck do you think it makes me feel, like fucking shit" Ruth became tense at the thought of treatment "So then there is other treatment like detersive therapy and drug therapy, the medication that I am on like others has side effects like confusion, hallucinations and increase night terrors"

"There must be something they can do?" Cheryl said concerned

"What can I do when my heads fucked, don't you get it Cheryl only I can do something about it" Ruth said watching the reaction on Cheryl's face.

"That's shit Ruth I don't believe that people can't help you, what about Kathy she must be able to help?" Cheryl said hoping for a positive reply.

"I can handle it and Kathy does help" Ruth said abruptly "It's a pity you can't deal with it after all you are supposed to be my girl friend".

"Ruth that's not fair I am not a psychiatric nurse you know" Cheryl pointed out upset by Ruth's remarks.

"I am going for a shower" Ruth said getting out of bed and walking towards the bathroom.

"That's it shut me out, do what Ruth does best close the door on the closest people to you" Cheryl shouted.

Ruth poked her head out of the bathroom door and looked at Cheryl, watching her sad eyes, Cheryl turned away and lay back on the bed.

"I am dealing with it myself; I can't let you into my head or my nightmares" Ruth said tearfully "Please try to understand that".

Ruth began to wash away the blood from her hands and legs which occurred during her sleep, fighting the ghosts that had been chasing her. She began to realise that issues hadn't been resolved and that the demons were still medaforacle speaking in her head. She had to address the facts one at a time a methodically from her childhood onwards, usually this can be achieved by counselling but she had to form a therapeutic relationship with her based on honesty and trust. Counselling was a specialised area and people who take on this role have to realise that they are dealing with someone's life, past, present and future. Ruth knew this and she was also aware of her own experiences and dealing with them, this meant starting from her childhood to adolescence and to the present. Ruth could appreciate Cheryl wanted to help her through this and when she returned to the bedroom she apologised and agreed to keep her proverbial door open and expose her tormented soul. Also as in any relationship the nice thing of an argument is the making up as Ruth did very well, this is why Cheryl loved her so much. Perhaps Cheryl sometimes caused an argument in order to make up with her, Cheryl was very passionate and became aroused by aggressive behaviour. Ruth became aroused by more visual displays of eroticism which she kept between her and her partner, suffice to say no bars were withheld in that department.

Ruth did seek help if only to please Cheryl, she went through several counsellors until she met Sharon who immediately noticed a pattern in Ruth's life linked to her past. Ruth wanted to meet her real mother Sarah, but knew she couldn't due to her untimely death, so Sharon suggested that she wrote to her instead. Ruth felt a little awkward about this at first and with Cheryl's help compiled a letter that she thought Sarah would appreciate. This was a very emotional moment for Ruth and Cheryl did as she promised by supporting her, she would make suggestions but not put words into her mouth. Ruth spent hours thinking and writing, screwing paper up and throwing them in the bin. Then she thought about Pamela and her relationship with Sarah, Pamela would often discuss her mother right from the time she said how Ruth looked like her. If only they had grown up together sharing their mother's affection, spending time in the park, at the cinema or any other family event. All those birthday's and Christmas's would have been wonderful and so magic, opening presents being taken to Santa like other children. Pamela never knew about having a sister and yet Ruth was always there, somewhere and then when they had a relationship that was another issue to deal with. Making love to her own sister even though she didn't know the facts was that so wrong of course when she found out it was too late. Pamela had died leaving another gap in her life and Ruth had a breakdown at this stage unable to face the world that had taken away her girl friend.

Ruth sat in front of the mirror putting on her make preparing to attend her counselling session with Sharon, suddenly she saw Colin in the mirror it was his reflection looking back at her making his face up wearing a dark wig and mimicking her, he then held up his knife and cut his own throat similar to his actions in the toilet prior to his death. Ruth dropped her mascara onto the table and noticed blood; she examined her arm and saw a cut with blood dripping onto her make up bag. When she looked back up the image had vanished and so she gave a sigh of relief and continued to apply her make up.

Ruth drove towards the hospital where Sharon met her and took her to a quiet room in was bright inside and the window was open, a gentle breeze drifted in with the scent of fresh summer flowers. Ruth sat comfortably opposite Sharon then remembered what happened in a previous counselling session when Sheila was the counsellor, she was hit on the head from behind and couldn't explain why. Ruth thought that Sheila could feel or see Pamela and that maybe she was defending her from harm, seeing Sheila as a threat because she had been given Ruth's diary to read that contained personal events from her childhood and teen years. She tried not to believe that Pamela's ghost was protecting her as she would be deemed as silly or mad, but her sister Emma had seen her and others.

Ruth produced the letter that she had written to her mother Sarah and showed it to Sharon.

My dear mother Sarah,

I would love to have known you and shared so much in your life, I feel a loss although I never knew you, and this will be the biggest regret of my life.

Sometimes my heart aches and I don't know why, sometime a tear fall and I start to cry. I want to hug you and tell you I care and tell you I love you and that it wasn't fair, to leave me out of my life bringing up my sister Pamela.

I know you had problems your illness with M.S and that you concentrated on Pamela's career, but did you ever think of me so far away. Apparently I resemble you in looks at least I can't say about my personality, but its said to be unique. We have both had our troubles and you died a horrible death, I wish I could have saved you. The people who hurt and murdered you are dead they you were avenged in the end, my poor sister Pamela died avenging your death.

I would like to say much more but I feel proud that I am your daughter I learned about your life and the love of Pamela's father Kevin. He was a brave soldier who you loved dearly.

Mother I have to inform you that I am a lesbian, you may not like this but it's part of me and I have a girl friend called Cheryl who I love very much, in fact I love her as you loved Kevin, please be happy for me, take me in your

arms and kiss my forehead and tell me you love
me, its all I want from you just for you to say
you love me.

Love from your daughter Ruth

Sharon tried to hold back her tears, she was good at hiding her emotions but this letter beat her to submission. She began to cry and Ruth grabbed the tissues on the table and handed her the box, Sharon took a tissue then apologised

"I am sorry here's me crying and yet you are the person that should be upset" Sharon said wiping her eyes.

"It's okay really" Ruth replied crying herself

"Nothing has ever touched me like that letter" Sharon continued "You are a very brave lady".

"I survive and live to tell the tale" Ruth explained

That very night Ruth began dreaming again but this time she dreamt that she met her mother who was holding the letter that Ruth composed. She was smiling and Pamela was sat beside her asleep on a couch, she beckoned Ruth over and patted a place beside her opposite Pamela.

"Hello Ruth" She said sweetly "I have read your letter and I wept it was so moving, you must have spent hours writing it"

"I did because I wanted you to know how I felt and about my life" Ruth replied

"Child you know I have thought of you all my life and continue to follow you even now" Sarah said stroking her hair.

"But you never contacted me or saw me" Ruth said sadly

"Ruth you must know that Laura kept me informed and it would have broken my heart to see you, Laura wanted a child but was unable to have any she became ill and then Diane brought you up". Sarah explained

"You were my greatest loss along with Kevin, but I was unable to cope with you as well as Pamela, I have left you a jewellery box with a few items such as a letter, a few items of jewellery and a porcelain mask as memories of me" Sarah looked at Pamela "See how your sister sleeps, so calm and peaceful even in death".

"Will she wake?" Ruth asked

"Yes eventually and then she will visit you wherever you are" Sarah said trying to shake her to wake up.

"See how she still sleeps, now promise me Ruth that you will live the rest of your life with a positive attitude, love Cheryl as I loved Kevin and never regret anything". Sarah said watching Pamela wake up and Ruth standing to leave.

"Oh Ruth don't be a stranger come to me whenever you want to, or whenever you have a problem" Sarah said vanishing with Pamela.

Ruth woke up with a feeling of ecstasy, she felt really good and positive about the future and when she returned to her counselling session with Sharon, she related the dream to her. Sharon interpreted the dream as coming to terms with her past, she was referring to her mother and the missing love. But Sharon could also see that Ruth was also unloading her guilt about Pamela being her sister and their relationship. But also she had built up the strength to conquer all her fears and be a stronger person inside.

The most amazing thing was that Laura contacted Ruth telling her about a jewellery box that she forgot to mention at Diane's funeral belonging to Sarah and left to her dear daughter Ruth only to be given to her after her death. It was also to be kept secret from anyone else in case the truth about Ruth was revealed.

Laura took it to Ruth the same day and all the items that were mentioned in the dream were in there. Ruth was bewildered at the contents, a letter for her, a ring, a necklace and a small porcelain mask which was slightly cracked.

The letter read:

My dear Ruth,

You don't know me but I am your mother, as Laura has probably told you my name is Sarah. I was forced to give you up and this will be one of the biggest regrets of my life, as Laura will confirm I have always asked about you and I did meet you once when your step mother Diane was walking you to school. You looked so much like me I cried for a week afterwards and never forgot that moment.

I have to tell you that you have a sister called Pamela who looks more like her father Kevin; he was my only true love who was killed in action as a soldier in the British army. I never wanted to lose him for anything although he was married; I committed a sin and paid dearly for it.

I am sorry that I couldn't care for you myself but circumstances wouldn't allow, but I love you dearly and one day I hope to be reunited with you in heaven. I leave you jewellery and a cracked porcelain mask to tell you life is not always perfect and you will experience problems on the way. God bless you my dear daughter.

Fondest love from your mother

Sarah

Ruth read it over and over again trying to make sense of it, the only thing that she couldn't truly comprehend was the verse about the jewellery box as she only knew about that in her dream. She even told Laura about it and described the contents before she had even opened it, as if she actually visited by her mother in her dream.

Ruth had a number of strange dreams after this and started to write about them trying to find answers to her life, the most profound was that of a woman called Martha, she named the dream Martha rest in peace.

MARTHA REST IN PEACE

It was a hot summers day in a small town near in the greater Manchester area, Where Martha lived with her husband Paul and children, John aged ten, Anthony aged eight and Gillian who was four years old. Martha was a thirty-eight-year-old lady fairly slim with short brown hair. Martha worked as a care assistant in a local residential home for the elderly, although she did this she also banked at a local hospital as an auxiliary nurse. Martha was considered a happy woman who was hard working and enjoyed being with her family. She used to arrange family days out to many places.

However, despite her healthy lifestyle and strict exercise regime it did not prepare her for the events that were to follow. One morning as she was hurrying to work, she rushed across a busy road and was hit by a speeding car, she was killed instantly. Martha felt cheated as she was so young and had planned to do so much with her life, she saw a bright light but refused to move into it, she was not ready and refused to let her spirit move on. Instead she decided to look for a body to live in for a while and live a little longer in order to stay close to her family. But she had difficulty controlling her spirit as it drifted into the hospital following her physical body attached like a magnet. Eventually she became totally detached; she was still avoiding the light that would lead her to her final destination. Her spirit continued to drift through the hospital until she found a host; the woman's name was Jessica who was a patient on a local psychiatric ward. Jessica was suffering from a form of personality disorder and had frequent psychotic episodes her condition was brought on by past traumas.

Martha had realised that she had drifted into Jessica's body but was unaware who she was or her diagnosis as a psychiatric patient. As she entered Jessica's body she began to react with a displaying rage and appearing to have a convulsion. This was witnessed by staff and patients as they looked on and noticed chairs being thrown and shouting like someone possessed. This was in contrast with the catatonic episodes previously displayed where she would appear rigid standing in front of the television and transfixed on the screen. She was restrained and sedated before being taken to a padded cell with white padded walls and a crash mat on the floor. Martha's spirit took a while to adjust and Jessica became dormant inside her own mind, it was as if Martha was switched on and Jessica turned off. Jessica always had dark rings under her eyes and a permanent stare, where Martha had bright blue eyes, clear and without any hint of darkness, her complexion was also good and unblemished. She remained in the cell for a while but Martha was confused as she didn't realise exactly what had happened. She entered the body during a traumatic event and was not aware of being in Jessica's body until she was put in the cell. It was like she had woken up looking at white walls and thought that she had been arrested, maybe held in a police cell. However, when she saw the staff come in to take her away, she soon realised what had happened.

She was in this body and couldn't break free; she had begun

to regret not walking into the light. When she reached her room she saw a reflection on a mirror and began to examine Jessica's face, starting with the eyes with their dark rings and then her spotty complexion.

"Bloody hell" She exclaimed.

Even her body was slimmer and she had smaller breasts although they were firmer and shapelier. Martha was trying to adjust to her situation when a nurse knocked on her door and entered in a cheerful manner.

"Hi Jessica how are you?" she said

"I am okay" Martha answered

"Well that's good, better than we have seen you I must say" She continued.

"Excuse me but who are you?" Martha asked confused.

"I am Ruth your nurse" Ruth replied

"Oh nice and where am I?" Martha asked looking around the room.

"Ward 35 on the mental health unit" Ruth explained "Don't you remember anything?"

"No nothing at all" Martha said looking at Ruth who was a young thirty-two-year-old nurse with beautiful big brown eyes and long brown hair tied back as we know. She was very attractive and appeared very attentive as she spoke to Martha, but then it was Ruth's dream so she invented the characters from her mind.

"You look different somehow have you done something with

your hair or is it something else" Ruth asked "I know it's your eyes, they appear brighter and less dark"

"Really" Martha said looking back into the mirror.

To Martha's surprise Jessica's eyes had changed, they were more like her own and her complexion had altered slightly.

"I have used a new foundation cream and less eye make up perhaps" Martha said smiling.

"We have a ward round tomorrow perhaps we can look at you going home" Ruth said positively.

"I hope so" Martha agreed.

The next day the ward round was scheduled for ten o'clock in the morning Martha was the second patient to be seen in front of a panel of four people. They consisted of Psychiatric Doctor Geoff Gilbert, RMN Ruth, O.T Karen and a student nurse called Wendy. Martha sat bewildered by these people all looking at her and watching her reaction to the questions that she was being asked.

"Jessica" Dr Gilbert said smiling

"I am Martha" Martha said sharply in a strange tone.

"Martha?" Gilbert asked

Martha thought about what she had said and corrected herself in her next sentence and Ruth was looking at her shocked.

"Sorry I was joking, thinking about the personality thing" Martha looked at each one in turn and smiled.

"So Jessica, how do you think your doing?" Doctor Gilbert

continued

"I am fine; you know feeling well and hoping to go home". Martha said.

"What do you think your parents will think of this?" Dr Gilbert asked

"Pleased I hope" Martha looked at their faces each looked shocked at her response.

"Pleased that I am well and resuming my life" Martha continued.

"How much do you remember about the accident?" Dr Gilbert asked

Martha was confused, how did he know about her accident was she showing through Jessica's body, could they see Martha?

"Geoff I think that I should point out that she remembers nothing" Ruth explained "We were talking earlier and Jessica can't even remember her twin sister Olivia"

"Oh so you don't remember fighting with your brother Alan and pushing him off the bridge? Dr Gilbert asked.

"No nothing I must have been traumatised by it" Martha explained hoping that Dr Gilbert would accept her explanation.

The ward round was very positive and they explained about her sister Olivia taking care of her, she would care for her and a community psychiatric nurse (CPN) would visit regularly.

Later that day her twin sister Olivia visited she escorted

Jessica to a table and sat offering her chocolate and fizzy pop (soda) Martha looked at her and smiled.

"You look really well Jessica" Olivia said smiling back "You're smiling and seem so happy"

"I feel well" Martha replied.

"But you're not eating your chocolate" Olivia said disappointed

"No I have gone off chocolate and pop" Martha said pushing the chocolate across the table.

"But you love chocolate and coco cola" Olivia seemed to behave oddly and hated Jessica refusing the things that she had brought for her.

"At least you're talking" Olivia said looking around her and feeling vulnerable amongst the patients.

"This place gives me the creeps it's horrible and I will be glad to get you out of here" Olivia said nervously.

"Its okay" Martha replied

"They say you're coming home soon" Olivia said "You can stay with me"

"That's nice but why you?" Martha asked wondering about Jessica's parents.

"You know, because of what you did, mother and father have never forgiven you" Olivia explained. "I know it was an accident but Alan died, you were seen pushing him off that bridge".

"Why did I do it?" Martha asked

"You were mentally unstable and you flipped, I tried to stop you, but you raced forward and pushed him hard during an argument", Olivia kept looking down as she was explaining the situation to Jessica. Martha was unsure of Olivia's story as she wouldn't give her eye contact while discussing the accident.

Later she went off the ward and when she had left the building she removed her mobile from the back pocket of her jeans and contacted her boyfriend.

"Craig how are you?" She asked him

"Olivia, how are you?" Craig replied

"Fine" Olivia replied

"How's Jessica? He asked

"Different, she was behaving oddly for her" Olivia said worried.

"Does she remember what really happened?" Craig asked concerned.

"That's what worries me, she will remember and tell someone" Olivia said nervously.

"If she is staying with us, maybe she won't say anything" Craig said trying to re assure Olivia "You may have pushed Alan but she's the mad one".

The time came for Jessica to be discharged from hospital under the care of Olivia, Martha was relieved as she was able to visit her own family although they wouldn't know who she was at least she was able to see them. She stayed at Olivia's apartment for a few days before venturing out to where she used to live. Olivia and Craig were inquisitive as to where she was going but didn't want to draw attention to themselves. They followed her to the crematorium and then went back home, Martha was attending her own funeral, she sat at the back of the room watching the service and wanting to go over to her family in order to comfort them. But she knew that in Jessica's body it would be a mistake not to mention a little weird. She sat and cried all through the service one of the family noticed her and commented to another.

"Who is that young lady?" she asked

"Probably someone from where she used to work" Another relative replied

"She must have been close from the way she's acting" she said concerned.

"Well she was popular" The lady replied.

After the service was over, people gathered around the flowers that were sent and began reminiscing. Martha stood in range to hear some of the comments and then stood near her husband and children hoping to speak to them.

"May I say how sorry I am for your loss" She said to her husband Paul

"Thank you" Paul replied

"You look familiar do I know you?" Paul asked

"No I don't think so" Martha replied

The children looked at her and smiled, Martha wanted to hug them especially the youngest Gillian. It was so difficult for her to control herself but she knew she had to in order to remain close to them. Inside her heart was breaking, so she decided to leave the crematorium and head back to Olivia's house.

Three weeks later she was looking for work and noticed an advert in the local newspapers for a children's nanny. By sheer coincidence it was at her home and the person advertising was her husband Paul who needed help. Martha applied for the job and was successful and so she became a nanny for her own children. The time passed and she the family became close to her, she was thrilled by this even though she was living in Jessica's body, she was still close to them.

Olivia was pleased that Jessica had a job but she was still concerned that Jessica would remember the truth about the accident and tell Martha's family.

Months passed by and Martha was getting closer to her family, she was invited to family trips out and Gillian invited her to her fifth birthday party. Martha knew what Gillian would like for her birthday, the type of cake and party theme. She decorated the one room in one theme spending a lot of money on each item, baking snaky food and organising party games with relatives. Aunty Thelma (Martha's sister) was very impressed and worked closely with her even providing music that Gillian liked.

All was going well, the party was being enjoyed by everyone, a lot of children attended and some parents helped, Martha got to know some parents as herself, but others knew Jessica from her picking Gillian up from school.

"I can't get over the fact that you know so much about Gillian" Thelma said

"Well it's all about learning and observing your children" Martha said smiling.

"You have a very mature head on your shoulders" Thelma said smiling back.

"I suppose so" Martha said watching Gillian dance.

"You seem a bit like Martha in your ways" Thelma observed

"Do you think so" Martha replied dying to tell Thelma the truth "You know"

"Yes" Thelma said expecting Jessica to reveal some big secret.

"Nothing" Martha replied knowing that it was futile to say anything.

Martha was experiencing more problems as Paul was getting g fond of Jessica and even spoke about them going out together for a meal. Martha had to step in and kept trying to avoid the subject and dealing with keeping her head together in a literal sense, after all she had to hope that Jessica would remain dormant. This was not just for her sake but Jessica's too as she was mentally unstable and could have a relapse, this would put Martha in an awkward situation and prevent the truth from coming out about Olivia. Although Martha was unaware of Olivia's situation she was in a position to help Jessica, she just needed time to help her.

Time passed and Martha was beginning to feel the effects of being inside Jessica's body, her spirit was weakening and Jessica was waking up. She was collapsing at times and acting oddly, she was losing control of Jessica's body, although she had introduced a healthier lifestyle with diet and exercise. She could not last inside this body for much longer after all it was never supposed to happen this way, she needed to cross over. Maybe she had fulfilled her destiny or accomplished tasks by helping Jessica and taken care of her family in her own way.

Paul and Thelma suggested that she saw a doctor as she was unwell, they noticed her collapsing and were worried about her.

One night Martha collapsed onto the bed and heard a voice in her head, it wasn't very clear at first and then it seemed muddled. She looked in the mirror and noticed her eyes changing.

"Where am I" Came a voice

"Who is this" Martha asked

"Jessica, who are you?" Jessica asked

"Jessica, are you there" Martha asked "I am Martha"

"Where are you?" Jessica said worried

"I am inside you" Martha said hoping not to startle her.

"Are you one of my personalities?" Jessica asked

"I am a spirit" Martha explained the full story to her, hoping that she would understand.

"My god you're actually inside me?" Jessica asked Martha.

"Yes, but listen tell nobody about me and follow my instructions" Martha said felling weak.

"Alright what do I do?" Jessica asked

"Your sister killed your brother and you were blamed for it" Martha explained.

"Olivia, but why did she do this?" Jessica asked

"Probably inheritance" Martha hesitated "But you can reveal the truth"

"How?" Jessica asked

"Be strong and trust me" Martha felt united with Jessica's mind.

Later that day Olivia entered visited the house where Jessica was working and pretended to be Jessica, she wanted to know how much they knew about Alan's murder. It seemed that the boys found out and Martha had explained the truth to them. So she took out a carving knife from the kitchen draw and attempted to stab John, his brother Anthony grabbed her from behind and they struggled. John was injured and Anthony also got stabbed, Paul entered the room and Jessica came in with the police.

Paul looked at Olivia and shouted.

"Jessica" he stopped and turned towards Jessica "Who are you?"

"I am Jessica" Jessica said smiling

"No I am Jessica" Olivia said trying to convince everyone that she was Jessica.

Jessica showed everyone the scars on her arms "This is from self-harm; I have been in hospital for this"

"I have seen these scars before on Jessica" Paul said pointing to her scars.

With that the police arrested Olivia and Paul hugged Jessica the children also made a fuss of Jessica. Later the police discovered the facts about Alan's death and Jessica was reunited with her parents. As for Martha she became detached from Jessica, her spirit was seen to disappear from Jessica's body by Paul and the boys, she spoke to Gillian saying goodbye and then entered the light. Martha's spirit has passed over accomplishing one good deed, she had not only reunited Jessica with her parents but destroyed the unwanted personalities. Jessica was cured and Martha was in a happy place. Which Ruth could relate to as she awoke and wrote the story as it is now, giving it a happy ending and making her feel happy.

MANCHESTER PRIDE

It was a glorious summer's day in Manchester and people were preparing for the annual event that showed the world that all people are equal and deserved to be noticed. I refer to the Manchester Gay pride festival which was notably the best parade ever. Ruth had been involved in some of the preparation work and encouraged her girl friend Cheryl and her own sister Claire to join in. It was without saying a spectacular event with many people either helping with the event or supporting the cause in some way. Ruth was dressed as a cat woman, Cheryl was dressed as wonder woman and Claire was bat girl. The parade began and Ruth was cringing as she walked through the crowds, at least when she was on the cat walk modelling she was above the crowd and parading up and down. Claire realised Ruth's dilemma and clung hold of her arm as they marched around. There was no trouble and the atmosphere was amazing, everyone felt comfortable transvestites dressed in beautiful frocks and no one seemed out of place. After the event they went into the bars and continued to party there, Ruth spent a lot of time discussing life styles with a few transvestite friends. They were remarking on how the parade was so colourful and how everyone worked so hard to make Manchester pride so successful. The facebook page showing all the events and photographs included a photograph of Ruth with Cheryl and Claire. It was one of the happiest days of Ruth's life being with people that she felt comfortable with, genuine people who were not afraid to be themselves.

Ruth had to fight to for her freedom and let people know that she was gay, it was a hard struggle convincing family and friends about her sexuality, now people were beginning to respect her, realising that she was genuine and sincere. Her life was all about being an individual and living her life as she really wanted to be. This day was all about that, she saw happy faces around her, people dancing and singing with love in their hearts and a kind regard for their fellow man. Ruth never wanted to rebel, neither did she want to mock others such as religious leaders or the media, rather they attacked Pamela and herself for being models and exploiting their sexuality, displaying their lesbian relationship in public. In reality they were forced to expose their sexuality to the public and they were ridiculed because of it. Ruth's ex boyfriend Malcolm the known psychopath saw them on television and became angry, he searched for them in order to kill them but killed others instead. This led to his brother Frank seeking Ruth and also causing mayhem all because of Ruth being a lesbian and standing up for her rights in public.

BROKEN WINGS AND LOST SOULS

A car races along a quiet road, being chased by a truck. It was traveling around hairpin bends and the two women in the car were frantically trying to shake off their pursuer. The truck hits the car once and almost causes the vehicle to leave the road; having failed the attempt the truck makes a second attempt to knock the car over the cliff. The car came to a halt and the driver of the truck revved the engine ready to ram the car and make a final attempt to knock the car over the cliff. The truck suddenly moved forward heading for the car everything seemed to go into slow motion.

One of the woman shouted, "Ruth put your bloody foot down!" she shouted.

"I can't it won't fucking work Cheryl," Ruth replied.

"We are going to die!" Cheryl shouted.

Suddenly the car moved forward and the truck raced forward over the cliff the driver was thrown clear as the truck hit rocks and exploded. After this took place Ruth explained that she had seen her former diseased girlfriend's ghost in the rear mirror and swore that she had saved their life. After she said this a man with an axe began smashing the car and trying to cut them to pieces. Moments later Ruth woke up and found blood on her legs and parts of her torso. Lying next to her was her girlfriend Cheryl fast asleep and unaware of Ruth's condition. After a while she too awoke and immediately noticed Ruth and the blood.

"Shit Ruth what's happened, have you been having nightmares again?" Cheryl said concerned.

Ruth nodded "Yes about Frank chasing us, but he survived the crash and came after us with an axe," Ruth said shaking.

Cheryl gave her a hug and kissed her on the cheek; she was aware of her nightmares and self-harming in her sleep. She knew how to deal with things although Ruth was the psychiatric nurse, Cheryl had learned a lot from her over the years that she had known her.

"You know that Franks dead don't you?" Cheryl said smiling.

"Yes of course," Ruth replied.

"We saw him die and so you're safe Ruth," Cheryl said.

"I know he died it's just me being silly," Ruth admitted.

Ruth got out of bed and headed for the bathroom; she stepped into the shower and washed away the blood from her body. She then washed her long dark hair and slim body; she then got out of the shower and put on her bathrobe. Cheryl had gone into the kitchen; she was making breakfast when Ruth appeared.

"How are you now?" Cheryl asked.

"Better thanks," Ruth replied, "Mm I love the smell of fresh toasted bread."

"Heaven to me dear," Cheryl replied.

"Kathy is picking me up for work," Ruth said.

"She is a good friend and colleague to you," Cheryl said.

Ruth had her breakfast and got ready to go to work; she kissed Cheryl and left the apartment. Kathy was waiting for Ruth in her car outside; she seemed worried as she sat gazing at the street ahead. Ruth rushed to the car and opened the door looking at her fair-haired friend and smiling cheerfully.

"Morning Kathy," Ruth said.

"Morning Ruth are you okay?" Kathy asked.

"Yes thanks are you?" Ruth replied.

"Yes I'm fine," Kathy said trying to hide her true feelings.

They arrived at work in time to get warm drinks before taking report from the night staff, a lot had happened to report and each patient was mentioned. The acute psychiatric ward was active with a variety of mental illnesses from bipolar to schizophrenia, all what Ruth termed as lost souls. People who have lost their way, people who need a sense of direction, ones who need help providing positively and not negative ideas. She had battled with Kathy to promote changes within the system of mental health, they had been friends for years and Kathy had supported Ruth through many problems.

After the ward round, the staff separated for a while concentrating on various aspects of the ward. Ruth and Kathy shared the drug round ensuring that each patient went to the serving hatch for their medication and then finding those who were in other areas. Observations were important and some patients were on special observations due to attempted suicide or misconduct. The corridors were busy with patients walking to or from their bedrooms; some were doing bizarre things, which was normal on an acute psychiatric unit. A patient called Alison was admitted because of postnatal depression, she would walk up and down the corridor quietly and sit in her room. Jessica had bipolar and was just going through her mania rushing down the corridor noisily and making fun of others. John was a schizophrenic who was having trouble managing his audible hallucinations using headphones in an attempt to drown them out with music.

Caroline who was suffering from clinical depression was having electric convulsive therapy (ECT), which Ruth attended and found it awful to watch, but it seemed to work as Caroline showed signs of improving. The need to shock someone in order to bring them back to reality seemed a little barbaric in today's society with all the drugs and various therapies, but as it still worked to a degree it remained an active treatment. Ruth never experienced it herself when she went through her depression, but her own history of mental illness stemmed from her child abuse or as she describes it, the dark and solitary place. She had been abused as a child and experienced mental and physical abuse from her former boyfriend Malcolm who was himself a psychopathic killer. He was responsible for the death of her girlfriend Pamela who was later discovered to be her sister.

They shared the same mother Sarah but Pamela died before her cousin Laura revealed the facts to Ruth.

Kathy was acting strange as she went about her duties on the ward as head nurse, it was unlike Kathy as she was so efficient and led the team successfully.

Ruth noticed that she was rather sharp at times and worked

alone most of the day. Her whole behaviour was out of character for her, but she was reluctant to discuss what was wrong with her at this time. Ruth noticed her enter the kitchen and followed her hoping to get some answers from her and ease the tense atmosphere that was caused by her behaviour.

"Kathy what's wrong?" Ruth asked her.

"Nothing really," Kathy said abruptly.

"Come on you can't fool me, I fucking know you," Ruth said snapping back.

"I said nothing now leave it Ruth," Kathy insisted.

"But you have been acting odd today which is unlike you," Ruth said concerned.

"I am busy so let me get on," Kathy said leaving the kitchen.

Later that evening Kathy had dropped Ruth off at her apartment she had hardly spoken on the way home and merely said "Goodnight," and drove away. Ruth went straight into her apartment and was greeted by Cheryl.

"Hi Ruth how are you?" Cheryl said embracing her.

"I'm fine just a little tired," Ruth admitted.

At that moment the phone rang and Cheryl answered it.

"Just a moment," Cheryl said offering the phone to Ruth. "It's for you."

"It's probably Kathy she's been acting oddly today," Ruth

said holding the phone to her head. "Hello," she said expecting to hear Kathy's voice.

"Hello," came a deep voice that startled Ruth.

"Do you know who this is, can you tell the voice?" the man continued in a deep voice.

"Who is this?" Ruth asked looking at Cheryl in bewilderment.

"Don't tell me you have forgotten me already?" He continued.

"It's Frank," He said in a menacing voice.

"No it can't be, is this some kind of sick fucking joke?" Ruth shouted.

"You wish bitch," Frank said laughing.

"Just stop bothering me you sick fucker," Ruth screamed down the phone.

That night Ruth had a nightmare about masks and skulls floating about. Ruth was dressed in a fashion costume with her girlfriend Pamela walking down a catwalk as they did in the fashion shows in the past. Pamela suddenly vanished and Ruth was left facing these masks alone, one mask came away from a face revealing her ex boyfriend Malcolm then another came away revealing his brother Frank. Ruth ran in slow motion trying to get away from them, but she eventually was captured and they attempted to pull her apart. She struggled free but fell backwards into the skulls; she tried to get up being pulled down into the skulls that were leaking blood. Eventually she got up but was stabbed by Frank and hit on the head with a baseball bat that Malcolm held firmly, he swung it once more and Ruth fell down.

Ruth awoke panicking and finding it hard to breath, she had hit her head on the cupboard door and Cheryl was attempting to calm her down.

"Ruth you're ok!" Cheryl shouted.

Ruth took deep breaths blowing air out and holding her chest as if her heart was going to explode. She became cold and clammy, the sweat pouring from her; gradually she calmed down and hugged Cheryl.

"What the fuck," Ruth said somewhat disorientated.

"Did you have another nightmare Ruth?" Cheryl asked.

"Yes this time with Malcolm and Frank, when will it end?" Ruth said shaking.

"But Frank and Malcolm are dead," Cheryl said.

"I helped kill Malcolm with Pamela," Ruth said. "But Frank I spoke to him last night," Ruth said rocking on the bed.

"But we saw him die," Cheryl insisted.

"No we saw the truck go over the cliff that's all," Ruth replied.

"Yes and the truck exploded no one can survive that," Cheryl explained.

"I can believe anything from those crazy bastards," Ruth appeared very upset with tears in her eyes.

Ruth got out of bed and opened the curtains slightly; she looked across at the park entrance. "He's out there somewhere and he's after me," Ruth knew that he would pursue her it was just a matter of time before he would plan his next move.

Ruth was due to commence work the following day, she had not heard from Kathy, which was unusual as she often rang or called into her apartment, but today Kathy was on the late shift. Ruth had a busy day with a long ward round, Dr Geoffrey was in a chatty mood which meant that the round was even longer. Ward round on a mental health ward took place in a large room with all the disciplinary team present, this consisted of the psychiatric doctor, the registered mental health nurse (R.M.N), an occupational therapist and sometimes a community psychiatric nurse (C.P.N). The occasional patient was due for discharge and plans needed to be put in motion. The patient was going back into the community to live amongst people who probably wouldn't understand their illness and could treat them badly. A proper plan of action was required if the discharge was to be a success, this could involve a temporary stay in a small house with others in similar situations. They would have someone watching over them, observing their capabilities in managing finance, caring for themselves and being compliant with medication. The problem of relapse was so common in the community causing patients to return to the ward and requiring further treatment. Ruth had seen this many times, these are what they term as revolving doors, or Ruth's lost souls that required nurturing.

When Kathy arrived on shift Ruth was ready to hand over to her, the morning had proven fruitful and quite eventful judging by the general activity. The patients appeared restless and you feel the tension in the atmosphere as if something was going to blow.

"Ruth, are you alright?" Kathy asked.

"Yes I just keep getting nuisance phone calls," Ruth replied.,

"Really, don't let it bother you" Kathy said. "I get them too."

"From Frank?" Ruth said surprised.

"No, why that's impossible this guy must be an impostor?" Kathy said shaking her head.

"Maybe," Ruth replied confused.

"He is dead you saw him die remember?" Kathy said prompting her.

"Yes I saw the truck blow up so he fried," Ruth said pondering.

"Like a lobster," Kathy said laughing.

"It's really not funny," Ruth said frowning.

"Ok sorry, but he can't be alive can he?" Kathy said trying to reason with Ruth.

"I wish I could share your confidence," Ruth said adjusting her hair tying it in a pony tale with a brown bobble.

"Try not to think about it, you have been through enough lately," Kathy said stroking her arm.

Later that evening Ruth and Kathy went out for the evening joined by Cheryl, Sheena and Gloria. Ruth had invited them over to give them some good news; she was gleaming that night because all her friends were present. Her sisters Emma and Claire were present too; also keen to hear her news.

"Now that you are all here I wish to announce to you that Cheryl and I are engaged and we are having a civil wedding."

Everybody cheered and applauded the surrounding tables also responded mostly positively by clapping. There were a few negative comments mainly by the homophobic people in the room; these were the ones to be ignored. One was heard to say 'How ridiculous whatever next.' Ruth never missed an opportunity to comment. "Ignorant bitch who the fuck does she think she is?" Ruth said aloud.

"Ignore her she's daft, hard up for a shag, try me or Ruth have some lesbian sex baby!" Cheryl shouted.

"Now girls concentrate on your wedding," Kathy advised.

"Oh yes my white dress, with frills, flowers and lace, I shall look such a fucking lady," Ruth said twirling around.

"What are you wearing Cheryl?" Gloria asked.

"I am wearing a blue dress with sparkling sequins and white laced cuffs," Cheryl added.

"I would like to get married," Sheena said looking at Gloria.

"Err, forget that babe I am straight," Gloria said laughing.

At that moment Angela walked in and immediately went over to Ruth and kissed her "Congratulations thank you for the phone call, I made it after all," Angela said.

Tara appeared at that moment "Do you need a photographer Ruth?"

Ruth stood up and ran towards her excitedly "Tara, how nice to see you."

"Angela told me about your wedding and I thought great Ruth is tying the knot at last," Tara said happily. "And I mean it I do insist on taking the photographs."

After hours of discussion about the wedding everybody parted company and went their separate ways, Ruth went back to the apartment with Cheryl, Emma and Claire. Claire wanted to speak to Ruth in private so they elected to make a drink for everyone, during the time they were in the kitchen Claire confided in Ruth.

"Ruth despite the fact that your real mother is Sarah, I still class you as my sister" Claire said

"Claire you are my sister, so what's the problem?" Ruth asked

"Well I am unsure about my sexuality; I don't know if I like men" Claire said bewildered.

"Who all have to find our own way" Ruth said

"But how do we know if it's the right way?" Claire said worried

"You will know it takes time to know for sure, but the feelings inside tell you where you need to be" Ruth explained "Just don't think a bad experience as a child makes you gay" Ruth explained "Child abuse is a bad thing and it is easy to blame every man for one bad bastard, but date others and experience heterosexual relationships first then you will know".

"Thanks Ruth you're the best" Claire said hugging her.

"Your welcome sister" Ruth said smiling.

"Ruth, are you working tomorrow?" Claire asked

"No why?" Ruth said inquisitively

"Lets go on a shopping spree" Claire said excitedly

"Sure that sounds nice" Ruth said with a finger on her lips "Shhh don't Cheryl to think I am spending our wedding money.

The next day Ruth and Claire left for the city, Cheryl had left early to go away on an art trip preparing for an exhibition called 'Life in a jar' based on a book by Stephen Sutton the idea was to take an ambiguous title and draw, paint or create anything around the title. Cheryl chose a jar with a human model inside symbolising restriction or limitations, over a hundred artist contributed to this exhibition. This made Cheryl feel good and that she had something to offer the world, it also gave Cheryl a sense of worth and achievement.

Meanwhile Ruth was enjoying her shopping spree looking around many shops and buying clothes, shoes and hats. Ruth and Claire were very close and enjoyed every moment of time together, shopping, eating out and drinking together. Then Claire led Ruth into a tattoo shop so that Claire could have a tattoo of a butterfly on her foot. Ruth sat looking around the studio at the many designs, and then she noticed an angel, which reminded her of Pamela.

"I would love to have that on my shoulder" she said "It would be a memory of Pamela".

"So have it" Claire said encouragingly

"No I shouldn't" Ruth replied

"Why not it's a good idea" Claire said

"Ok I will" Ruth agreed, "Does it hurt?"

"Honestly Ruth you have been through so much and you're worried about a little discomfort". Claire laughed

On their way around the shops they met Laura, so Ruth told her the news about her wedding but Laura wasn't sure how to take the news. Laura wasn't quite sure what she thought about Ruth's relationship with Cheryl, she was never sure about the lesbian thing as she called it. She loved Ruth but not her lifestyle, but Ruth's idea was to love people for who they are. She believes its all about people being genuine and truthful to themselves, people respect honest people and who can do exactly what they want to do as long as it doesn't physically harm others.

Claire stayed with Ruth that night they drank wine and spoke until two am then they slept until late morning. They went for breakfast in a nearby café on the way they met one of the neighbours called Paul a slim and well-spoken man who specialised in law. He sat staring at Ruth on another table, he hardly moved for at least half an hour; Ruth felt a little uneasy and soon left the café.

A week passed and she met Paul going into the same café, Paul seemed embarrassed at seeing her and spoke to her.

"Ruth I wanted to see you" Paul explained

"So now you've seen me" Ruth said suspiciously

"Ruth don't be like that" Paul said feeling hurt

"Well what do you expect, the last time I was in here you just stared at me" Ruth said looking at him and pointing her finger "How did you expect me to react, I find that creepy" Ruth was determined to get her point over.

"I'm sorry but to be honest I really like you" Paul explained

"Oh so its love or lust then" Ruth said bluntly

"No not at all I think you're beautiful and in my opinion it's a waste, you being a lesbian" Paul said sincerely

"Well to you it must be you being a full blooded heterosexual male" Ruth began to feel relaxed in his company.

"I guess that I will have to continue dreaming. Paul said jokingly

"Well to be honest you do make me laugh" Ruth admitted

"As long as I amuse you" Paul said smiling

"I suppose if I were honest if I was heterosexual you would be the man for me" Ruth said smiling back.

"Really, then I feel better for that" Paul said

"I am pleased about that Paul honestly" Ruth said with sincerity.

They left the café, hugged and kissed and then parted Cheryl had just got back from her trip and saw them kissing.

Ruth returned to her apartment surprised at seeing Cheryl, she noticed the expression on her face and the cold reception that she received.

"Cheryl what's wrong" Ruth asked

"I notice you have a tattoo" Cheryl said

"Yes an Angel" Ruth said "Do you like it?"

"I suppose that is Pamela?" Cheryl said sharply

"She was my sister you know" Ruth said angrily

"And your lover" Cheryl said

"Oh I see you're jealous of a dead person" Ruth said

 "What are you up to I saw you kissing Paul outside the café, do you know what you want or which way you want to go?" Cheryl said

"For fuck sake Cheryl he is a friend I don't like him that way and as for Pamela "I explained about her being my sister and now I think of her as my sister ok" Ruth said pacing up and down.

"I suppose so" Cheryl said sitting on the settee

"If you don't trust me what is the use marrying me, I am honest and true to you but you don't trust me".

"I am sorry but maybe I am insecure" Cheryl admitted

"Well don't be so fucking stupid and grow up" Ruth said walking towards the bathroom.

Cheryl left Ruth to calm down before knocking on the bathroom door, she had been crying and felt guilty making accusations about Ruth.

"Ruth please come out" Cheryl pleaded

There was a silence Cheryl was worried that Ruth had done

something stupid so she knocked on the door again.

"Ruth!" she shouted

The door was unlocked and Ruth appeared looking tired and upset, she looked at Cheryl who looked sheepish at her, with her eyes pleading forgiveness.

"I am really sorry Ruth I have been so foolish" Cheryl said

"It's ok let's get a drink" Ruth said

"So is the wedding still on?" Cheryl asked

"Of course" Ruth replied walking forward with her arms out to hug Cheryl.

They had supper then went to bed and continued their conversation cuddled up together in bed.

"Ruth I know you have been through more than anyone else I know and endured as much as anyone can, but try to let me in, please". Cheryl said

"I will try to do so honestly" Ruth said "But sometimes my head is fucked and the ghosts from my past haunt me, I am like a bird with broken wings". Ruth explained. "So how do I help my lost souls?"

"Let me mend your wings so that you can deal with your lost souls" Cheryl offered.

"Ok heal me and let me learn to love you deeply" Ruth said kissing Cheryl on the lips and caressing her body.

"Let me release the demons from your head and the badness that lurks within" Cheryl said kissing her back.

The next morning Ruth returned to work happily knowing that her future was planned and she had more to look forward to as she had a wedding on the horizon. She picked Kathy up from her house and headed to the hospital and the acute mental health ward that they had worked on for so many years together.

"Good morning Kathy" Ruth said

"Morning Ruth" Kathy replied

Kathy seemed distant again and was just nodding, as Ruth spoke none stop about her wedding all the way to the hospital. When they arrived Ruth spoke to Kathy in the staff room with others present.

"You know that I am getting married" Ruth began

"Think so Ruth you have told me every detail to date" Kathy said

"Well we want you to be maid of honour" Ruth said

"Don't you mean maid of dishonour" Kathy replied

"I said that last night" Ruth said laughing

"Cheeky bitch" Kathy replied

"Well will you?" Ruth asked

"Depends whether I am here or not" Kathy said

"Fuck off Kathy of course you will be" Ruth seemed puzzled by what Kathy had said.

Suddenly one of the staff commented

"A wedding for gays, how silly, a civil wedding they call it, I call it gays showing off, flaunting their sexuality". The woman said scornfully

"Well I'm not going" she continued.

"Who invited you?" Ruth asked

The woman bowed her head in shame as she didn't realise that she was speaking so loud and was overheard by Ruth. Kathy looked at Ruth as if she had spoken out of turn, but Ruth continued to speak to the woman.

"Well Kathy some people consider that their life is the only way to live, the pompous arrogant fuckers. Yes, I mean you Janet oh look Anna is back as Janet thinking she is perfect, the one who destroyed Pamela and now wants to destroy my relationship with Cheryl too". Ruth said angrily.

"Ruth not now please" Kathy said embarrassed

"It has to be said Kathy" Ruth continued "Bad mouthed bitch"

"Ruth!" Kathy shouted slamming her fist on the table.

Ruth looked at Kathy in shock "My god you're defending her against me"

"For Christ sake Ruth its not all about you, stop being selfish" Kathy looked angry and pale.

Ruth looked at Kathy in disbelief she tried to touch her on the arm but Kathy shrugged her off "Don't please" Kathy said coldly looking away from Ruth.

Ruth looked at the staff who were in the room, including

Janet and then walked out of the staff room slamming the door on her way out.

Later Kathy approached Ruth to apologise, Ruth was still upset not by being shouted at she was used to that, but by Kathy not defending her as she had done many times before.

"I am truly sorry Ruth" Kathy said

"Its fine" Ruth said

"No it bloody well isn't fine" Kathy continued, "I am not fine"

"What do you mean" Ruth said looking at Kathy

"I have a lump on my breast" Kathy said pointing to her left breast

"Shit no" Ruth said shocked

"I have known about it for months but couldn't tell you" Kathy said

"Why I am your friend" Ruth said with tears in her eyes

"That's exactly why, because I am tough, strong and dependable, well taking a look at the tough woman now" Kathy said with tears trickling down her face.

"Oh my god Kathy not you" Ruth hugged her and they both wept together,

"Now you have to be the tough one Ruth, the cancer has already spread and I will have to have treatment soon". Kathy explained.

"I am not hearing this, god I feel sick" Ruth said trying to keep strong.

"Come on Ruth I need your strength right now" Kathy held Ruth tightly

"Yes your right I must be strong for you" Ruth tried to control her emotions.

Ruth's mind was distracted by the activity on the ward Trevor who was by polar was going through his manic period dashing up and down the ward shouting. While Sally was repeating herself constantly saying 'it's me oh yes it's me'. Ruth and Kathy shared the drug round that morning, watching each patient take their medication correctly and not storing them in their mouth. Kimberly was prepared for her electric convulsive therapy (ECT) to jolt her back to reality.

Ruth tried to be a tower of strength for Kathy and avoided telling her of the repeated phone calls from Frank. She took Kathy to some of her chemo sessions and returned her home to her family but underneath she felt as if she was losing another mother figure that she adored even more than her stepmother Diane. Her rock and protector was ill and fading before her eyes and she couldn't stop this from happening. Ruth looked back on the many times that Kathy had helped her over the years. She had defended her when she went off with a patient called Pamela to do modelling and helped her back to nursing. She was there when Raven the schizophrenic tried to kill her and through much more. The clock was now ticking for her and Ruth felt helpless, unable to stop this deadly disease from killing her friend.

Ruth walked through the park with her mind drifting back to past events such as when they went out drinking, times at work with problem patients. But what was more important Kathy being instrument in helping her to recover from depression and become re-established on the ward as a qualified psychiatric nurse. Ruth remembered the special loving relationship they had with each other as friends, hugging each other in appreciation for what they did for each other. Ruth thought back to the battle between Raven and herself and how Kathy fought with her until the death of Raven who was killed when a branch landed upon her penetrating her body. Ruth stood by the tree where Raven died and visualised her last moments of life in this place in the park.

Ruth also was aware that Malcolm her ex psychopathic boyfriend murdered someone near here with a baseball bat. She thought about the disasters that occurred, due to Malcolm and his brother Frank in their attempt to kill Ruth. She thought of her brother and sisters and the dreadful childhood being abused and her dark lonely place in the wardrobe, where she hid many times from her abuser. Kathy had even helped her to cope with this in a way that no one else could. She showed Ruth how to think ahead and not dwell on past events, to act positively with a goal in mind. As she continued walking she passed an old man in a wheelchair they were heading towards the apartment building where Ruth lived. The man spoke to the girl but Ruth was too far away to here as she headed out of the park gates.

"That's Ruth" the man said

"You mean the one who killed your brother?" The woman asked

"Yes Malcolm and her apartment is this way" He pointed to

the apartment ahead.

Ruth walked to Diane's house, she was apprehensive about entering the house due to so many bad memories there. As she entered the house things came flooding back, such as the death of her so called father, the rows with her step mother Diane and Sister Emma, not to mention her abuse as a child.

Emma and Claire sat in the living room as Ruth entered, both greeted her with open arms, Emma's baby Lucy was in a carry cot by the settee.

"Aw how is Lucy?" Ruth asked

"She's fine" Emma replied

"So who's making a drink then?" Ruth asked cheekily

"I will I suppose" Emma said reluctantly

"I must use your toilet" Ruth said heading towards the stairs

She walked up the stairs and entered the toilet; after she had been she walked into the bedroom that she had as a child. Here was where all the abuse took place years ago, but it was like yesterday. The wardrobe that she used to hide in which she called her solitude of safety was still there old and tatty but the even the loose handle was never fixed. Ruth reflected back to the dreadful incidents that scarred her life forever, she became anxious and started to tremble. Her heart was pounding and tears trickled down her cheeks, she could smell aftershave and sweat mixed together which to her was a ghastly odour that made her rush to the toilet and vomit. The fact that she could visualise in her mind all the horrific scenes from her abuse made her stomach churn and caused her such pain.

At that moment Claire appeared and comforted her, she too had been abused in this house and in the same room.

"Are you alright Ruth?" she asked

"Yes just the past rearing its ugly head like an unwanted growth" Ruth replied.

"I know what you mean" Claire said concerned

"It fucks my head right up" Ruth continued.

"Me too" Claire said looking back into the room.

"They ought to knock this place down, either that or burn it down" Ruth said angrily.

"We should move somewhere else, too many bad memories" Claire said

"Emma won't move you know that, she was never affected by abuse" Ruth said bitterly.

"Then let's talk to her and explain how we feel, I am sure David will agree". Claire insisted.

They went downstairs and began to discuss it with Emma

"No way, I am not leaving this house no matter what happens" Emma insisted

"But just think of all the bad memories Emma" Claire said trying to reason with her.

"For fuck sake Emma see reason" Ruth said annoyed

"This is your idea Ruth and you don't even live here" Emma snapped back at Ruth.

"Yes but I do" Claire said.

"So why don't you live with Ruth" Emma said holding the baby "Lucy is going to grow up here".

"This fucking place should be burnt down" Ruth shouted

"And me in it I suppose for wanting to be here" Emma said becoming tearful.

"Don't be like that I only want what's best for us all as a family" Ruth said

"Family is that what you call us, Mother died because of you" Emma said then realised what she had said in anger. "Sorry I didn't mean that".

"No but you said it" Claire said defending Ruth

"I have to go I will catch you later, Kath needs me" Ruth said walking towards the front door.

"How is she?" Claire asked

"Very ill she's having chemotherapy, she's sick, tired and fed up". Ruth said opening the front door.

"If we can help let us know" Emma said concerned

"You have enough to do" Ruth replied walking outside.

Later that day Ruth was sitting next to Kathy's hospital bed with Gloria and Sheena, they were discussing wedding plans.

"So may I ask Ruth, who have you got to making your cake?" Sheena asked

"Don't know yet" Ruth replied

"We can organise that" Gloria said

"Really?" Ruth said surprised

"Yes a special treat" Sheena said

"With roses and colourful like your life" Gloria said laughing

"That's true" Sheena agreed.

"Cheeky lot anyone would think I am someone who lives the high life when I'm on an emotional roller coaster half the time with a fucked head" Ruth said.

"Language" Kathy said waking up.

"Sorry Kathy" Ruth said looking at the others.

Later that day Ruth was about to drive past Diane's house heading home when the road was blocked ahead. She noticed fire engines and an ambulance; suddenly she panicked and ran towards a crowd of people, Diane's house was on fire. Flames engulfed the living room and the firemen were busy trying to put it out, Ruth tried to fight through the crowd panicking. Suddenly she saw Claire and David, standing with blankets around them talking to police men.

"Where is Emma and Lucy?" Ruth shouted

"Still inside, they are upstairs" Claire said in tears.

"My god no" Ruth said putting both hands to her mouth.

Suddenly two firemen came rushing out just in time for the fire to spread upstairs; one was carrying a baby and the other supporting Emma.

At that point a police officer approached Ruth, he appeared

very stern.

"Are you Ruth?" One of the officers said

"Yes I am" Ruth replied

"Then I need you to come with me to the station" He continued

"Why what's wrong?" Ruth asked

"Someone answering your description was seen in the vicinity and one witness said that you started the fire" He said

"She didn't do it" Claire said in her defence.

The officers led Ruth past the ambulance where Emma was just entering in a wheelchair. Emma looked at Ruth and shouted coughing at the same time.

"Well you got your wish, the house is burnt down" Emma said then looked away.

Ruth remained silent and entered the police car, Claire joined Ruth while David went with Emma.

Ruth and Claire seemed to be in the interview room for a long time before two officers appeared doing their usual routine of good cop, bad cop questioning Ruth about the arson.

"Come on Ruth you were heard to have said 'I would love to put a torch to this fucking house and burn it down' those are your words aren't they?" The bad cop asked.

"You are very attractive a model on Television" the good cop said smiling.

"Did you say that?" the bad cop repeated.

"Yes I did but I didn't do it" Ruth insisted

"But you had a bad time in that house, nobody blames you for doing it" Good cop said.

"So just admit it" Bad cop said

"Someone was seen there like me and I was at the hospital visiting a friend" Ruth explained.

"An alibi but you could have arranged for someone else to do it" Bad cop continued.

"For fuck sake you are really annoying me, I said that I was with a sick friend and besides I would never cause a fire or my family harm".

The interview continued for half an hour and then Ruth was released from the police station and they both went to Ruth's apartment.

That evening Ruth's phone rang it was Frank; Ruth put the phone on speaker for all present to hear.

"Ruth how did you like the fire, this is just the start I am going to make you suffer for the death of Malcolm". Frank said in a wicked voice.

"You're a tucking maniac" Ruth shouted.

"I sent Raven to kill you; she failed so I sent others and will keep on sending them until your dead". Frank continued making threats towards Ruth.

"Stop all this madness you sick bastard". Ruth said

hysterically.

"Am I getting to you Ruth?" Frank said sneering.

"You think you're so fucking clever, but you're just a sick shit" Ruth shouted even louder.

Everything went silent then the call ended, Ruth raced into the bathroom to be sick. Emma was present to hear Frank along with David, Claire and Cheryl, all witnessed that Frank was behind the arson.

The police were informed about the phone call and they began investigations into Frank's whereabouts. At least Ruth was no longer a suspect and could continue helping Kathy, nursing her through her last days.

Kathy was transferred to a hospice and Ruth arranged time off work to care for her there, she insisted on washing her and making her look nice. She was in and out of consciousness during the day and night, but Ruth never left her side.

Ruth knew her death was immanent, it was just a matter of days or hours who knew as some people say it was in the hands of god.

But one sunny morning Ruth was looking out of the window at the swaying trees and the cherry blossom, when a bird fell to the ground with its wing broken. Ruth was unable to reach it as it struggled to get up, it was helpless and defenceless like so many people she had seen before including herself. At that moment Kathy opened her eyes and tried to focus on Ruth, she smiled and tried to speak despite all the morphine that she was receiving through a syringe driver.

"Ruth you are in my dreams; I am pleased you are with me"

Kathy said in a slurred manner.

"I am with you Kathy; I will never leave you" Ruth said gripping her hand

"Bless you for taking care of broken wings and lost souls" Kathy continued

"You are the same Kathy, you mend wings and care for lost souls" Ruth said trying to hold back her tears.

"God I am scared Ruth; I am afraid to die" Kathy admitted.

"Please don't be let yourself sleep in peace" Ruth felt tears trickling down her face as she notices Kathy passing away.

Kathy took her last breath and Ruth put her head on her chest and wept. At this moment Sheena and Gloria appeared and tried to consol her.

"No not Kathy, my rock, my dear friend she can't die I need her" Ruth shouted

Sheena and Gloria cried too as the nurses rushed forward to assist, Ruth refused to let go of Kathy clinging hold of her dead body. Eventually Sheena and Gloria managed to free her from Kathy and escort her to a quiet room.

"Why didn't god take me, I did ask him, I did" Ruth said even though she doubted Gods existence.

Gloria just held Ruth tightly in her arms, while Sheena held Ruth's hand they sat for a moment while the nurses took care of Kathy behind some screens.

"I saw a bird with a broken wing, it was outside the window" Ruth said pointing to the window.

"Someone put it in a box" Sheena said "They took it away".

Kathy's funeral took place at the same crematorium as Diane's and Pamela's funeral, many people attended as she was loved by many people. Ruth reflected back to Diane's funeral and remembered Laura telling her about her real mother Sarah, if only she had known her and shared her love. Varied arrangements of flowers were present, displayed outside with the names of friends and relatives who rarely saw Kathy. Kathy was a private person as the vicar pointed out, she chose her friends carefully but loved Ruth like a daughter and often protected her.

Ruth returned to work she sat with Kimberly who was discussing her depression and how the E.C.T had benefited her, she was about to go home and seemed happy. Trevor dashed past them going through another manic moment, he was shouting expressing strange thoughts. Alison a rather large lady who suffering from schizophrenia sat staring into space with headphones on, evidently blocking out the voices in her head. These people were Ruth's lost souls and she loved them, she in fact would be lost without them and she often imagined Kathy was with her to share them and their needs. Kimberly looked at Ruth for the first time since her admission, she used to just put her head down and look at the floor. She had beautiful blue eyes that were once dull, now they seemed to sparkle like diamonds in a ring.

"Thank you for helping me" Kimberly said touching Ruth's hand

"Your welcome, I hope all goes well for you" Ruth said smiling.

"I was sorry to hear about Kathy" Kimberly said looking at Ruth's large brown eyes "You are so attractive like a model".

"Yes well let's not go there" Ruth said laughing.

"Ok I won't peruse that" Kimberly laughed for the first time since admission.

Trevor raced around them laughing in a more mocking way, then coming out with a random comment. While Alison removed her headphones and walked out of the room.

It was a week later when Frank began to call Ruth again, he became more intense with his calls and sent one of his friends to damage Ruth's car. It was the woman who resembled Ruth who burnt down Diane's house, unfortunately for her the police were watching the car at the time. They anticipated another attack on Ruth or her family and sat in a car near to Ruth's apartment, seeing the woman starting to smash the windows with a metal bar rushed over and arrested her. They took her to the police station and questioned her, after a while she confessed and with little persuasion she told the police where Frank lived.

The police raided Frank's home discovering photos of Ruth and her family displayed on a wall, with details of addresses of family and friends. He had planned out events and even named who was allocated to harm or kill each person, but the final plot was for him to shoot Ruth with his own gun near the park. What was more worrying it was planned for that day, even the time was displayed for nine o'clock. One of the officers reached for his radio and alerted the police control centre.

Frank was waiting for Ruth to appear; he was sat in his

electric wheelchair hidden under a tree. He was hiding in the shadows and called Ruth as she was passing close by, holding his gun out aiming it at Ruth's head.

"Ruth" He shouted

Ruth looked at him and froze on the spot, she was completely motionless as she noticed his finger on the trigger. Her whole life passed before her as she waited for him to squeeze the trigger and shoot her dead.

"I have waited a long time for this Ruth, now at last I can kill you" Frank said in a menacing voice.

"Go ahead kill me after all you have ruined my life" Ruth said with her arms out

"I just want to see you suffer a moment longer, plead for your worthless life" Frank gloated "I want to see the fear on your face and" Frank was interrupted by Ruth

"Fuck you, you're just a sad pathetic bastard like your brother Malcolm, go ahead shoot me" Ruth shouted in rage, but quivering inside.

"That's it now you die" Frank said pulling the trigger

A loud bang echoed down the street and Ruth fell backwards with the impact of the bullet, Franks wheelchair then raced forward and his eyes widened as he saw a bus heading at great speed before him, the impact knocked the chair across the road and he catapulted out into the road. He was hit by another heavy vehicle and was crushed under a wheel, his stomach burst open and his intestines spread across the road. When examined the police noticed that his head had been decapitated at some point. Blood was everywhere and even present in the wheelchair indicating that he must have been injured when the bus hit him.

Ruth lay on the ground Cheryl and Claire raced over the road to reach her, the police were already there examining her.

"Is she dead?" Claire asked.

Ruth opened her eyes and looked up at the crowd of faces everything was blurry, but she did see Pamela in the background.

"No she was lucky just a shoulder wound" one of the policemen said

"Ouch it fucking hurts" Ruth said touching the blood on her clothing

"She's ok she's cursing and swearing as usual" Cheryl said smiling.

"Are you her family?" An ambulance driver asked

"Yes we are" Claire said smiling at Cheryl

"You go to the hospital with her Claire" Cheryl insisted.

In the ambulance Ruth continued complaining on the journey to the hospital

"Fuck it hurts can't you give me anything for pain" Ruth said rolling her eyes

"Ruth please they are doing their best your lucky to be alive" Claire explained

"Oh am I, is that so you try getting shot" Ruth continued

"At least you're alive" Claire said annoyed

"What makes you think I want to be" Ruth shouted

"You selfish bitch" Claire said slapping her across the face.

"Claire" Ruth said holding her face

"Well sorry but we all love you" Claire said feeling guilty.

Ruth became silent and looked at Claire holding her hand.

"I love you Claire" Ruth said smiling

"Piss off Ruth" Claire said smiling back

Emma was at the hospital greeting them in, David hovered in the background pacing up and down. Once the bullet had been removed from her shoulder Ruth was taken to the ward to recover. She was surrounded by admirers and each one was discussing the civil wedding, they spoke about dresses and cakes.

Emma sat with Ruth alone at one point discussing family and where they had been given a home.

"Ruth you were right, there were too many bad memories there especially for you and Claire, so we have a new home and it's really nice" Emma explained.

"I am pleased for you Emma" Ruth said smiling

"So what happened with Frank" Emma asked.

"I don't really know Emma, things happened so fast" Ruth sighed "He held the gun up shot at me, but I swear that I felt someone push me hard on the shoulder and I fell to the ground. My other shoulder was burning and I felt a sharp pain then passed out". Ruth explained.

"You were pushed?" Emma asked

"Yes definitely pushed, then I came round and began hallucinating seeing Pamela". Ruth said bewildered

"Christ Ruth you did see her she saved your life, she is your guardian angel" Emma insisted.

"No way" Ruth dismissed her

"It the only explanation and apparently Frank's electric chair went out of control into the road" Emma explained

"So what happened to him?" Ruth asked

"Don't worry the twat is dead, his body was torn apart by two vehicles" Emma went on.

"Nice way to go for a psycho" Ruth said bitterly.

Emma hugged Ruth and kissed her gently on the cheek

"Well sister lets home all your problems are over" Emma said sincerely

"Look ahead and continue dealing with my lost souls at work and look forward to the wedding with my friends and family".

The civil wedding took place as arranged many people attended and shared the happy day with Ruth and Cheryl, it was published in all the gay magazines and even mentioned on the local news. Ruth returned to the ward feeling Kathy's presence as she went about her routine, taking care of her broken wings and lost souls.

CRACKED PORCELAIN FULL STORY

THREE

REMEMBER ME

This is the continuing story of Ruth Ashley a mental health nurse who experienced so much throughout her career and personal life. Ruth is in a car crash with a reporter from Criminal World magazine, following an investigation of cursed mirrors. They had returned from Mexico and were driving home in England when the cars brakes failed; they swerved off the road and landed in a ditch. Ruth awoke and found herself in a strange place with someone that she least expected to meet, Pamela, she was once her lover, but later she discovered that she was her sister. Seeing her convinced Ruth that she was dead and the following events made her think about her past. It seemed like a recap on her life as Pamela reminded her about many traumatic events such as being abused as child, and facing abuse from a relationship. But Ruth became confused later when she saw a vision of herself nursing an old woman whom she thought resembled her, she wondered if this was her in her own future. The question had to be asked was she dead or experiencing an epiphany of her life in the form of spiritual manifestations that were visiting her either in a strange environment or in the depths of her mind. Time alone could tell her what she wanted to know and how to deal with it rationally, as Ruth was trained to do. Ruth had realised that cursed mirrors were not the worst thing she had ever challenged as she battled her way through her own epiphany.

REMEMBERING PAMELA

It was a warm afternoon all seemed calm, there was no sign of life the wreckage of a car lay at the foot of a hill. Inside the car sat two women one in the front passenger seat and one in the driver's seat. Both women were covered in blood and not moving, they appeared not to be breathing and their eyes were closed. Suddenly a bird appeared, it was a tiny sparrow which rested on the roof and then flew into the sky.

Ruth Ashley a psychiatric nurse began to open her glazed hazel eyes and gazed through the window ahead, blood was trickling down the side of her head and down her left cheek. Her long dark hair was wet and scraggly; she appeared pale and confused as her mind relived the accident that caused her to be here.

She remembered the conversation between Fiona and herself as they were travelling home from a difficult experience in Mexico concerning cursed mirrors. Fiona a reporter who worked for Criminal World and Ruth was assisting her with her work. They had just dropped a friend off home in the north of England called Pepper.

Fiona and Ruth took Pepper home, returning her to her family. They stayed overnight and then headed south in order to drop Ruth off in her apartment, but as they journeyed home they came across rough weather and Fiona was experiencing problems with her brakes.

"Ruth I am so glad you helped to lift the curse," Fiona said.

"We all played our part Fi," Ruth replied modestly.

"I suppose we did, but what team work!" Fiona said smiling.

"Well if ever you need me again let me know," Ruth offered.

"I will hold you to that Ruth," Fiona promised.

"I have to say we were lucky to escape alive from that situation," Ruth said with relief.

"I can't believe you walked forward and told that witch Zyanya to help us!" Fiona said in amazement.

"I know I amazed myself with that one!" Ruth said smiling.

"The brakes have failed I can't slow down!" Fiona said panicking.

Fiona pressed again at the foot brake and nothing happened, she was unable to slow down and lost control of the car, she veered off the road and went rolling down a bank and crashing into a ditch. Fiona and Ruth appeared pale and lifeless, they sat with their heads to one side, there heads were bleeding. No one was in the area and the car engine was still running with smoke travelling through the air drifting across an open field with no sign of life, not even wild life. Everything remained still, the skies were empty and everything appeared dull as if the life had been taken from the earth leaving nothing but death as a legacy to the world.

Ruth returned to the present and saw a bright light before her it almost blinded her; she raised her hand in front of her in order to shade her eyes from it. It was the light people spoke of that you enter when your crossing over into another world or heaven. She could hear a voice that seemed to sing to her it was a strange but interesting voice that she recognised to be Kate Bush and the song was called "This Woman's Work." After a while it stopped and she took her arm away from her face, finding herself in a different place. She was in a bed in the middle of a brightly lit room, decorated with white and gold walls, cupboards and even the bedspread was white with a gold bedspread.

She gazed around bewildered by the sight. Then she noticed someone enter the door and sit on the edge of her bed, she was blonde and very beautiful like an angel dressed in white.

"Pamela!" Ruth said tearfully, "but you're dead!"

"I am here with you now," Pamela replied.

Pamela embraced her kissing her on the cheek and feeling her wet tears on her lips.

"It's so good to see you again," Ruth said sobbing.

"It's good to see you my love," Pamela said squeezing her tight.

Ruth gazed into her blue eyes and wiped her tears away with her hands, she paused for a moment feeling something trickling from her nose and dripping onto the pure white sheets.

"I thought I was dead so how am I bleeding?" she asked.

"It is something called temporal displacement you are between worlds not dead or alive, but in transit. Your condition will stabilize eventually and you will experience the next phase of consciousness," Pamela explained.

"What the hell does that mean?" Ruth asked wiping the blood from her nose.

"It's like being between two time zones and your mind being torn between them trying to adjust," Pamela said placing her hand on her shoulder.

"I found out about you and my real mother Sarah. Is she here too?" Ruth asked concerned, "I had a dream about her and I was given a letter from her."

"She knows and will see you presently but for now you must rest my sweet and sensitive sister Ruth," Pamela said, she was also shedding a tear for her sister.

Pamela stood up and walked out of the room, leaving Ruth lost and confused and reflecting back to the past. To the time when she first met Pamela on the psychiatric ward. It was when they were waiting for a new admission with other staff including Kathy. Ruth remembered Pamela's wild manner as she appeared on the ward handcuffed to a policeman and shouting obscenities, she calmed her down and befriended her not knowing that she was her sister and even began a relationship with her. But how was she to know that Pamela was her sister, it all ended in tragedy as Malcolm stabbed her to death. Ruth was reliving the experience and trying to make sense of her present situation, questioning why she was in such a place living in some kind of time zone or kind of limbo situation, was she dead or alive.

THE MATTER OF ABUSE

Ruth could never understand religion or politics and what made things worse was why God allowed people to die and for so much cruelty to exist in the world including abuse, rape and murder. She often prayed to God to make her fathers friend Ron stop abusing her and hid away in the wardrobe which was her dark solitary place of safety.

Ruth had many arguments with clergymen who pompously criticised Pamela and her for their sexuality, yet within their own faith people in position of office abused children and were protected by their flock. Ruth was more outspoken than Pamela and would not hold anything back, cursing and swearing at them as she expressed her opinion openly to one and all. Another problem that Ruth found was that people would do anything for their religion or God even kill, which was in conflict with her ideals or philosophy of live to love and love to live. Alternatively do what you want to do as long as it doesn't harm yourself or others; this is probably more accurate in Ruth's case.

Ruth once dreamt about an argument that Pamela and her had with a clerical group about the so-called abomination of homosexuality. Ruth shouted at them cursing their religion and their slant on the Bible.

"You load of fucking hypocrites!" she began, "bad mouthing our sexuality while you sexually attack children," Ruth scolded.

"Have you read the Bible on homosexuality?" one of them said pointing at her.

"Christ man you think the Bible is everything, do you think you rule the world with your religion?" Ruth said pointing at a cross on the wall.

"No, but I assure you God does and you are acting against God by your sexual promiscuity," he continued, "vile acts of sin and debauchery with you two leading the way."

"Well fuck you and your flock; we are in love and not shagging around thank you!" Pamela added.

"Listen to them cursing and swearing isn't that proof of how evil they are?" another clergyman said.

"You're enough to make a fucking saint swear with your idealist world and grandiose ideations, you would be happy in fascist society run by fascist leaders as has happened in history," Ruth said.

"Yeah the type of society that excluded anything, out of the norm," Pamela added.

"Well we know what the Bible says about you," a clergyman shouted.

"The fucking Bible is okay, but its people who misquote it, they twist words round, that's what you lot do," Pamela said pointing at them.

After Pamela commented the religious leaders looked at each other and when the audience applauded they left disgusted by what they had heard. This was quite common when Pamela and Ruth were together on stage amongst opposing parties such as religious leaders and politicians. They were used to being publicly attacked and criticized for their sexuality. When Ruth woke up she felt stronger as if Pamela had visited her in her sleep and instilled a sense of purpose into her. This was probably one reason that Ruth was on the road to recovery.

Ruth was joined by Kim who had died as a result of her eating disorder she merely sat in the corner of the room and rocked with a cuddly toy in her arms. Ruth was baffled by her presence and waited for Kim to speak; this took a while as Kim just wanted to stare into space. Ruth had seen photos of her, and Sheena discussed her occasionally.

"You did modelling didn't you?" Kim said.

"Yes a little but it wasn't for me, too much pressure," Ruth admitted.

"Yes I thought so, competing against others keeping my weight down," Kim revealed her unusually thin legs by lifting her dress.

"So you did this because of your job?" Ruth asked.

"Not just that, peer pressure, you have to have the right image," Kim explained.

"But my problem was nothing like yours Ruth!"

"What do you mean?" Ruth asked.

"Your abuse as a child," Kim said concerned.

"You know about that?" Ruth said with a look of shock on her face.

"We all know everything here, no one has secrets," Kim

smiled but in a more empathetic way. "So tell me about it?"

"The abuse as a child was from a man my father knew, we called him Uncle Ron. He was horrible fat and smelt odd with cheap deodorant which masked a wicked smell of body odour. He used to follow me to my room and start talking to me, being nice and friendly this was obviously to get into my knickers. I don't mean to be crude but that's what he was up to, touching my leg a bit like my father used to do. He was really creepy and the smell was intoxicating, he began by touching my leg and then went further to my private parts. He'd threaten me saying don't tell your parents it's our secret and they will get upset and throw me out or worse. I finally discovered that if I knew he was coming I would go out or hide in my wardrobe and stay in there for hours until he went. This was my dark and lonely place, or solitude of safety a secure environment from creeps like him; he was a monster and deserved to die. He was killed by a van his head was crushed like a melon; I saw it splatter all over the road!"

"God you must have been traumatised for years after he abused you?"

"Yes but it happened to my sister Claire and I didn't know until later, I could have prevented that happening if I had only spoken up," Ruth admitted.

"Ruth it wasn't your fault it was that monster, and your father to blame," Kim said.

"I suppose so, but I have always blamed myself for getting in that situation myself and for poor Claire."

"What about Malcolm?"

"He was nice at first charming, amusing and generous, but then he changed. He was very jealous of me; I had no friends because of him. It was like curfew I had to be in at a certain time and if I went out from work he would come and look for me. He would rant and rave, show me up in front of my work colleagues."

At that moment Kathy walked into the room, Ruth rushed over to hug her.

"I don't believe you're here and looking well!" Ruth said with surprise.

"Ruth don't let me distract you from your story, feel free to express yourself you are safe here," Kathy said encouraging Ruth.

"Well Kathy was there when he dragged me out of a pub, punched me and caused me to fall onto a wet pavement, 'Get up you stupid bitch' he shouted when we got home he tore my dress and then raped me. I tried to get away from him but he found me each time, I was always going to work with either, a black eye, bruised cheek or fat lip. Everyone said to leave him but I couldn't I suppose I loved him and he put up with my night terror activities like self harm or screaming. Who wants that kind of responsibility from a psychotic woman who was on the border of being sectioned, I was trapped and couldn't see a way out like Ron the monster scenario all over again but with the violence."

"Ruth you need to tell us everything let it all out, your anger, frustration, your emotions," Kathy said encouraging Ruth to give more of herself for some reason.

"No!" Ruth shouted. "Don't make me do this anymore."

"Ruth you must please it's for your own good," Kathy insisted.

"But it hurts Kathy my stomach is in knots and I feel sick," Ruth said clutching her stomach.

"Tell me," Kathy shouted.

"I am afraid, I am in pain, and I am fucking hurting!" Ruth shouted.

"You can't feel pain in this place," Kim said standing over her.

"I wanted to tell Malcolm how he hurt me and humiliated me, how he fucked with my head and raped my mind," Ruth stood up and began pacing and shouting back at both Kim and Kathy. "I hate you Malcolm you are the most evil man that I have ever met and I curse the day you were ever born. You have taken my body and defiled it, but I am the one who survived I am alive, my mind and body are free!"

"Now how do you feel?" Kathy asked.

"Fucking wonderful!" Ruth replied.

"Truly?" Kim asked.

"Yes at last I can breathe again and I have no pain the sickness has gone," Ruth said watching Kathy and Kim disappear.

"Kathy, Kim!" Ruth said confused.

At that moment Diane appeared sitting on the edge of her bed, she was dressed in a cream blouse and dark skirt, her hair was short and she sat smiling.

"Diane," Ruth said hugging her.

"Ruth my problem child who I love so much," Diane said softly.

"I never wanted to hurt you, but I brought so much trouble to your door."

"Nonsense Ruth I was joking about you being a problem when your father caused your anxiety and despair," Diane said bitterly.

"I hate that man he was evil," Ruth said agreeing with her step mother.

"You are my angel with clipped wings, my love I don't blame you for anything you were unfortunate being pursued by Malcolm, Frank and Raven."

"But Raven killed you I tried to get to you but I was too late she had already stabbed and killed you."

"No Ruth, what happened was not your fault, don't blame yourself, remember me in a positive way without guilt and remorse, I love you Ruth and I will be here for you always."

"Thank you mother," Ruth said relaxing.

"I think about Claire and Emma and I also don't blame you for Claire being abused. I do blame your father and that evil monster of a friend of his."

"I feel better now, love you mother," Ruth said watching her step mother vanish.

COUNSELLING

Ruth thought about her many occasions with various counsellors, she considered most of them as time wasters and not worth bothering with, sat with nice frocks and layers of make up. She considers these people as text book counsellors who had no compassion or true understanding of a patient's true feelings. They go through the motions but are like puppets being controlled by or driven by their master puppeteer. But the session became a little heated when Sheila made reference to her Father leading into her abuse.

But then she decided to continue again sitting on the edge of the seat.

"Let me tell you about my fucking father, let me tell you how he stood and let me get abused by my so called Uncle Ron, that's how much that bastard loved me!"

Sheila looked a little uneasy as Ruth was getting angry, "My father beat him up, half killed him when he eventually realised what this man was doing," Ruth took a breath and continued. "He wasn't even my real uncle just some friend of my fathers, who dared to abuse me and befriend the family, what a sick bastard."

Ruth could no longer hold the tears back, then suddenly vomited in the waste paper basket. She heaved and retched. Sheila reached for the panic button but changed her mind and picked up a box of tissues instead and passed it to Ruth.

"I'm sorry," Ruth said wiping her mouth with a tissue.

"It's ok," Sheila replied. "Is this how you normally react to this abuse?"

"You mean vomiting, shouting and swearing?" Ruth asked.

"Yes. It must be very distressing for you," Sheila said empathising.

"If I didn't puke, I don't know what I would do," Ruth said tearfully.

Sheila's eyes appeared tearful and Ruth was able to see the compassion in her face. Maybe she did understand her and that's why she didn't press the alarm.

"The puking is me reacting to the abuse isn't it?" Ruth said looking at Sheila and sitting with a more open posture.

"Do you want a drink of water?" Sheila asked.

"Yes please," Ruth replied.

"Do you want to continue?" Sheila asked looking at the time.

"Yes I do," Ruth said composing herself.

"I see," Sheila said.

"Well it's that or thump at the wall or slap the therapist!" Ruth said smiling.

"Well thump the wall, not me!" Sheila replied smiling.

Sheila handed Ruth a beaker of water, which Ruth took from her and sipped.

"That's nice, I feel better for that," Ruth said wiping the excess water from her mouth with a tissue.

"Listen Ruth, you know how it works, you're a professional psychiatric nurse for goodness sake," Sheila smiled and continued. "You're a good nurse by all accounts and a caring person and you've helped many people including Pamela."

"Yes, but I was responsible for her death," Ruth said putting the beaker on the table.

"Do you really believe that?" Sheila asked.

"Sheila, she ran in front of me when Malcolm came at me with a knife, then Pamela got stabbed in the abdomen." Ruth said pointing to her own stomach.

SEXUALITY

"Yes people think lesbian relationships are a fad and don't last, just women being silly, but if you've never tried it why knock it?" Ruth paused, "We understood each other, we may have been hormonal at times but the deep rooted love that we shared could never be compared to a heterosexual relationship, even the sex is different."

Ruth smiled and continued, "It's about kissing passionately and the warmth of two naked bodies entwined together, I really can't explain the rest but believe me its good!"

Sheila gave a cough to clear her throat and then began, "So Ruth when we spoke you were telling me about Pamela and that special holiday you had together."

"Yes I would say it was the best holiday that I had ever had, she used to wear a dark wig so that we were never recognised, because we were famous." Ruth replied.

"You spent a lot of time in the public eye?" Sheila said fidgeting with her pen.

"Yes with fashion shows and magazine advertisements, not to mention the media and their antics." Ruth said watching Sheila tapping her pen.

"The power of love show seemed particularly popular and raised a lot of publicity, good and bad I thought, how did you feel about that?" Sheila asked.

"I felt on top of the world like a Princess in a castle and it was so personal, all about us, Pamela and me." Ruth suddenly stood to her feet and demonstrated the moves on the catwalk. "Pamela taught me how to walk the walk and smile or use the correct facial expressions, we practiced to music." Ruth said sitting back down.

"And the costumes were good too?" Sheila said putting down her pen.

"Yes the top designers were present, offering such glamorous outfits and some quite bizarre ideas too!"

"What about your family, what did they feel about your modelling?" Sheila asked.

"Oh they hated it, in fact they hated everything I did, he didn't want me around," Ruth replied.

"Who do you mean, your father?" Sheila asked biting her lip.

"Yes him!" Ruth said sharply, "I hate him!"

There was a short silence during which time Ruth began thinking about her painful past, then she continued, "He hurt me, he really hurt me and I swore that no fucker would do that to me again both him and my uncle can both go to fucking hell!"

"How did they hurt you?" Sheila asked.

"With what they did, touching me, messing with my body thinking they could do this to me and not be caught, but my father got scared and decided to beat my uncle up covering his own tracks." Ruth paused for a moment to think again.

"But the evidence was there, all written down."

"Evidence?" Sheila asked.

"Yes too bloody right I kept a diary that no one knew about placed in a brown envelope in a draw hidden under some other items." Ruth said looking at Sheila's reaction.

"I wrote everything down, times and such when he came to me," Ruth suddenly went pale, "I feel sick, sorry I need to stop."

Sheila went to touch her to reassure her that she was fine, but Ruth suddenly jumped.

"Sorry, did I make you jump?" Sheila asked.

"It's ok, I just fucking freak out sometimes when anyone touches me, it just the way I am sorry," Ruth said.

"I understand," Sheila said smiling.

"Pamela understood me, she went through the same type of things, she was very beautiful with blonde hair and blue eyes and a lovely complexion and figure." Ruth stopped again to collect her thoughts. "Her mother Sarah brought her up as a single parent and introduced her to modelling from an early age, she was so perfect until she was abused by her uncle, her real uncle."

"She was special?" Sheila commented.

"Very special like her mothers' porcelain ornaments, that was before she was abused then she became damaged like cracked porcelain, imperfect, broken irreparable." Ruth said in dismay, "She was never the same after that, she was a happy girl turned sad by her abuser."

"Would you say that you were like her?" Sheila asked.

"Cracked porcelain you mean?" Ruth said hesitating; she thought about what Sheila had said and became tearful. "Yes I suppose so."

Ruth sobbed and repeated herself, "Cracked porcelain."

SAVED BY AN ANGEL

Ruth thought back to the many occasions when she was in danger and realised that she must have been helped in some way, like the time she was at her mother Diane's house, relaxing and supposedly in a safe place.

Ruth was sat watching television when a knock came at the door; she was hesitant but answered it eventually. To her horror it was her father who brushed passed her and entered the kitchen, he seemed angry and started shouting.

"What's wrong George?" Diane said concerned.

"It's being branded round at work that I am a paedophile, me that's a laugh!" George said.

"So you fucking well are!" Ruth shouted.

"It was you wasn't it, trying to get at me?" George shouted.

"No but I wish I had," Ruth said angrily.

"You nasty bitch I could kill you!" George lifted his fist at her.

Emma heard the shouting and entered the room, seeing her father she became angry but Ruth had already slapped him around the face and was fighting him.

"You bastard pretending to be so innocent, letting me suffer all that time in the hands of your fucking friend," Ruth shouted punching him in the face.

Emma pulled her off and tried to calm her down.

"The mad bitch should be still locked up why is she here?" George asked.

"Why are you fucking here you pervert?" Ruth said trying to get to him.

"Dad just go, you've caused enough damage," Emma shouted.

"She's caused the bloody damage slandering my name," George shouted being held back by Diane.

"She didn't, I did," Emma confessed, "I wanted you away from here and locked away for what you did to Ruth."

"You bitch my special Emma, how could you?" George was confused by Emma's confession.

He pushed Diane away and she fell to the ground hitting her head on the floor, in the confusion Emma saw a figure with a bright light around her brandishing a knife in her hand. The figure then thrust the knife into his chest and he fell to the ground in agony. They all ran to him except for Ruth who stood still staring at George lying on the floor. Emma ran to her mother who was dazed but not injured, Ruth walked forward almost in slow motion. She knelt by his side and saw his eyes staring up at the ceiling he was holding his chest.

"Is he dead?" Emma asked.

"Yes," Ruth replied.

"Did you see what happened?" Emma asked.

"Yes he must have had a heart attack," Ruth said her mind was detached from the situation as if she was having an outer body experience.

"No that's not what happened, it was Pamela!" Emma paused for breath then continued, "She stabbed him in the chest I saw it happen," Emma insisted.

"What?" Diane said holding her head. "She's dead!"

"No honest I saw her as clear as I see you now," Emma continued, "She stabbed him in the chest with a knife."

"Emma there's no knife and certainly no blood," Ruth said searching round the floor.

"I know what I saw, just like on the ward where you were," Emma was almost hysterical.

Claire appeared at the moment her father had collapsed and was found sat at the foot of the stairs almost oblivious to the whole event, as if she was detached from the situation. Whether or not she was in shock was not clear at this point, but she sat there even when the paramedics and police appeared in the hallway.

They all attended his funeral but no one mentioned any events that took place at the house. The fact was he was dead and could no longer cause the family any harm.

The family stayed together and hardly spoke to anyone else; they had found it difficult to trust anyone else because of the family abuse. In fact, the abuser their father's friend was at the back of the crematorium acting like nothing had happened. Ruth had turned around to look at the people who had attended; there he stood in a suit smirking. Ruth whispered to Emma.

"What the fuck is he doing here?" she said annoyed.

Emma nudged her mother and whispered to her, then whispered to Ruth.

"Let mum and I deal with him okay," Emma patted Ruth on the hand.

"Just don't let the bastard near me, or I will castrate the fucker," Ruth said angrily.

"In fact all men should be castrated," Ruth continued.

"Leave me at least one man for reproduction purposes!" Emma said sniggering.

Once the service was over everyone left the crematorium each shook the vicar's hand but Ruth who just waved in an odd fashion. They looked at flowers outside and walked past George's friend Ron, he smiled at them as they passed and tried to speak to Diane. Diane turned and faced him then spat in his face watching him wipe his face with a handkerchief looking so surprised at her.

"You dare touch my children again," she said angrily.

"She came on to me, I am the innocent party," he said covering his fat stomach with his coat and adjusting his glasses.

Ruth heard what he said and was being held back by Emma who also heard him.

"How dare you even say that you fat bastard," Ruth said trying to get to him.

Claire became very upset and grabbed hold of her mother, while Emma pulled Ruth away from trying to attack the man.

"Come on Ruth he's not worth it," Emma said.

"He's just shit under my foot," Ruth shouted, "Go on piss off pervert!"

"Let him go Ruth please your upsetting Claire," Emma pleaded.

Ruth walked on with the family and had almost got in the car when the man passed by her smirking.

"To think that I got arrested because of you and that other daft bitch," he shouted.

Ruth launched at him scratching his face and kicking him between the legs, suddenly by complete surprise Claire joined in kicking him in the head. Diane pulled Claire off and Emma jumped in Ruth's way. The police soon arrived and began to split everyone up Ruth was still swearing at the Ron.

"I hope you rot in hell you fucking pervert," Ruth shouted watching the police approach her. "It's him you want," Ruth said as one of them held her.

"Why did you let him go, you thick bastards."

A policewoman was holding her, "Now come on calm down," she insisted.

"Let me go he's a paedophile and he needs punishing not me," Ruth said struggling.

"Let her go," Claire shouted hysterically.

Diane had never seen Claire reacting like this before and didn't know how to control her. Claire was trying to reason with the police, explaining that Ruth was being provoked by her abuser's presence. Diane agreed with her and demanded that the police arrested him.

"He's the trouble maker, he abused my daughter," Diane shouted.

Ron looked at the family then the police, "The bitch deserved it, come on let me have all of you," Ron shouted approaching Ruth.

The police realised what was happening and two of the officers started to walk towards Ron who by this time was laughing and teasing the family with vulgar gestures. The police officers were taken by surprise seeing Ron's antics and stopped in their tracks.

Suddenly a van swerved out of control in the car park and headed straight towards the family, and then it changed direction and drove towards Ron. Ron moved backward to avoid the van; he tripped over the curb and landed in the road. No one was close enough to move him out of the way and he was hit directly in the head by the bumper of the van. He had no chance of surviving as his head smashed like a melon and blood splashed right across the road. Emma once again witnessed a glow of light coming from the van, which disappeared as fast as it came. She remained silent and just looked across at Ruth who was being held by a police woman, she then looked at Claire who was bent over by the pavement vomiting. Ruth was released by the police during the time the van hit Ron and ran to comfort Claire.

When the police reached the van they found the driver unconscious and appearing very pale with blue lips. It was later discovered that he had suffered a heart attack at the wheel and he died in hospital. Therefore, it was questionable whether or not Pamela was actually involved in this incident as Emma thought at the time. Although she could have steered the van away from the family and towards Ron, no one will ever know for sure. It is also questionable whether or not they would even believe her. But again it was another case of a man with no conscience who had suffered the consequences of his actions. Also was Ruth saved by a ghost or angel, or was it a coincidence. Ruth had remembered so much about Raven and Colin which disturbed her even more she had unresolved issues about so many things, from so many people she could feel the pressure in her head as if she was about to explode.

Ruth had sleepless nights reflecting back to her past, her therapy did help but the rest was up to her to deal with issues and move on for her own sake. Ruth knew that if she lived a hundred years she would still carry the inner scars of her past, but she needed to introduce her own coping strategies to deal with the occasional reminders of her former trauma. She had dealt with the shame, humiliation, self-disgust and embarrassment of the abuse. Also of the feelings of being contaminated, dirty and defiled, she spoke of guilt, blame and a debased self-image. So she had come a long way to recovery in this sense but she will never be separated by her night terrors or nightmares. Her years of avoidance and isolation had ended with the burning of the wardrobe and improved relationship with her mother Diane, but what also remained were those occasional feelings of anxiety and helplessness when she was reminded of her predator. The smell of aftershave, deodorant or people who resembled him, often music or the smell of nicotine made her physically sick.

Ruth got involved with a girl called Sammy who she considered a girl friend when Sammy just wanted a one-night stand as she was involved with another woman.

Ruth often went to the gay village in Manchester she went to a bar and saw Sammy, a butch lesbian was with her and she noticed Sammy making advances to Ruth just like the last time they met. She raced forward angrily and began shouting at Ruth, Sammy tried to stop her and the woman punched her in the face. She continued to head towards Ruth ranting and raving at her like a wild bull, beating Ruth up again she was saved by an angel or ghost.

RAVEN

Ruth thought back to Raven who had caused problems with her family. Raven was reported to be diagnosed as schizophrenic and had been arrested for the forensic attack of a blonde white woman who Ruth and Kathy knew as Sharon. All the ward staffs were alerted; even the other wards close by just in case they needed support. The fact that Raven was subjected to audible and visual hallucinations influenced her own judgement and she was unable to function clearly without these voices of command telling her to do things. She believed that God was telling her to hurt people and that he wanted to cleanse the earth from evil, demons or fallen angels that had to be destroyed. She was led to believe that some angels were deceptive they were wolves in sheep's clothing; they were usually blonde and wore virginal white gowns and spoke softly. Raven sounded quite credible too as she related her story to the police, community psychiatric team and other professional bodies, she presented as a frightening woman even her voice sounded chilling as she spoke low and gravely.

"Let me go you bastards!" Raven shouted.

Raven was even more dangerous than Frank and believed that he was an angel and that Ruth was a demon who deserved to die.

Both Ruth and Raven ran towards each other, Raven swung her branch and narrowly missed Ruth who swung her branch and hit Raven in the arm. Raven then made an attack on Kathy scratching her neck and part of her face, causing her to stumble and fall to the ground. Ruth went into a rage and hit her across the face, then punched her in the stomach. Raven fell to the ground and became very still for a while, at this point Ruth checked Kath's injuries. At that moment Raven recovered from her attack and headed towards Ruth her hands shaped like claws trying to scratch Ruth.

"I will claw you to death you evil bitch," Raven said knocking Ruth into the mud.

"Fuck you I will beat you this time," Ruth replied pushing her against a tree.

Raven came back at her and stumbled allowing Ruth to jump on top of her and grabbing her hair and pulling her down in the mud. They fought for a while until Ruth managed to break free from Raven's clutches and fall back onto the ground. Raven picked up another branch and rushed towards Ruth who noticed a figure above them in the trees, but found it hard to focus on her. A bolt of lightening hit a tree near them and a branch came crashing down on Raven. Part of the branch entered her stomach and pierced her left eye. Raven lay lifeless with her other eye staring up at the sky, and then blood began to ooze from her mouth. Ruth looked up at the figure in the trees and noticed her blonde hair and a radiant smile; this was clearly Pamela who was there to protect those she loved.

Another big problem for Ruth was a young man called Colin who was a transvestite killer who was calling himself a killer queen. Colin was dangerous because he wanted to be exactly like Ruth and killed any women who opposed Ruth in any way. He was obsessed with the music of Queen and with Ruth as a perfect woman, he actually wanted to be her and knew this was impossible unless she or he died.

SURVIVAL

Ruth had weird dreams probably due to her past and ward experience sometimes wished that she had remained a model like Gloria and Sheena. Sheena tried to persuade her to return to modelling and managed to get her on a few photo shoots with her. Sheena was stunning with her ginger hair and blue eyes and was so fit and healthy; she went to the gym and often went jogging with Ruth in the park. She took a good diet and drank vegetable smoothies, her skin was soft and smooth and her blue eyes sparkled. She didn't like Ruth at first, she saw her as the lesbian who stole the stage due to her sexuality, but warmed to her when she got to know the real Ruth.

Ruth thought about her counsellor Sheila and probably considered her as one who did understand her to a degree, she was upset about Kathy showing Sheila a diary of hers and that spoilt things a bit, and she was also surprised that Pamela made her presence known to her by hitting Sheila on the back of the head defending Ruth. Part of Ruth's survival hinged on the counselling sessions by Sheila.

Ruth thought that Sheila could feel or see Pamela and that maybe she was defending her from harm, seeing Sheila as a threat because she had been given Ruth's diary to read that contained personal events from her childhood and teen years. She tried not to believe that Pamela's ghost was protecting her as she would be deemed as silly or mad, but her sister Emma had seen her and others.

Sharon was her next counsellor who she admired as she felt that she had also experienced problems, she seemed to react to Ruth's situations as if they were personal. She also shed a tear at some moments when Ruth related her abuse to her and went into detail.

Ruth produced the letter that she had written to her mother Sarah and showed it to Sharon.

> *My dear mother Sarah*
>
> *I would love to have known you and shared so much in your life, I feel a loss although I never knew you, and this will be the biggest regret of my life.*
>
> *Sometimes my heart aches and I don't know why, sometime a tear falls and I start to cry. I want to hug you and tell you I care and tell you I love you and that it wasn't fair, to leave me out of my life bringing up my sister Pamela.*
>
> *I know you had problems your illness with M.S and that you concentrated on Pamela's career, but did you ever think of me so far away. Apparently I resemble you in looks at least I can't say about my personality, but it's said to be unique. We have both had our troubles and you died a horrible death, I wish I could have saved you. The people who hurt and murdered you are dead they you were avenged in the end, my poor sister Pamela died avenging your death.*

I would like to say much more but I feel proud that I am your daughter I learned about your life and your love of Pamela's father Kevin. He was a brave soldier who you loved dearly.

Mother I have to inform you that I am a lesbian, you may not like this but it's part of me and I have a girl friend called Cheryl who I love very much, in fact I love her as you loved Kevin, please be happy for me, take me in your arms and kiss my forehead and tell me you love me, its all I want from you just for you to say you love me.

Love from your daughter Ruth

That very night Ruth began dreaming again but this time she dreamt that she met her mother who was holding the letter that Ruth composed. She was smiling and Pamela was sat beside her asleep on a couch, she beckoned Ruth over and patted a place beside her opposite Pamela.

"Hello Ruth" She said sweetly "I have read your letter and I wept it was so moving, you must have spent hours writing it!"

"I did, because I wanted you to know how I felt and about my life," Ruth replied.

"Child you know I have thought of you all my life and continue to follow you even now," Sarah said stroking her hair.

"But you never contacted me or saw me," Ruth said sadly.

"Ruth you must know that Laura kept me informed and it

would have broken my heart to see you, Laura wanted a child but was unable to have any she became ill and then Diane brought you up," Sarah explained.

"You were my greatest loss along with Kevin, but I was unable to cope with you as well as Pamela, I have left you a jewellery box with a few items such as a letter, a few items of jewellery and a porcelain mask as memories of me," Sarah looked at Pamela. "See how your sister sleeps, so calm and peaceful even in death."

"Will she wake?" Ruth asked.

"Yes eventually and then she will visit you wherever you are," Sarah said trying to shake her to wake up.

"See how she still sleeps. Now promise me Ruth that you will live the rest of your life with a positive attitude, love Cheryl as I loved Kevin and never regret anything," Sarah said watching Pamela wake up and Ruth standing to leave.

"Oh Ruth don't be a stranger come to me whenever you want to, or whenever you have a problem," Sarah said vanishing with Pamela.

The most amazing thing was that Laura contacted Ruth telling her about a jewellery box that she forgot to mention at Diane's funeral belonging to Sarah and left to her dear daughter Ruth only to be given to her after her death. It was also to be kept secret from anyone else in case the truth about Ruth was revealed.

Laura took it to Ruth the same day and all the items that were mentioned in the dream were in there. Ruth was bewildered at the contents, a letter for her, a ring, a necklace and a small porcelain mask which was slightly cracked.

The letter read:

My dear Ruth

You don't know me but I am your mother, as Laura has probably told you my name is Sarah. I was forced to give you up and this will be one of the biggest regrets of my life, as Laura will confirm I have always asked about you and I did meet you once when your step mother Diane was walking you to school. You looked so much like me I cried for a week afterwards and never forgot that moment.

I have to tell you that you have a sister called Pamela who looks more like her father Kevin; he was my only true love who was killed in action as a soldier in the British Army. I never wanted to lose him for anything although he was married; I committed a sin and paid dearly for it.

I am sorry that I couldn't care for you myself but circumstances wouldn't allow, but I love you dearly and one day I hope to be reunited with you in heaven. I leave you jewellery and a cracked porcelain mask to tell you life is not always perfect and you will experience problems on the way. God bless you my dear daughter.

Fondest love from your mother

Sarah

Ruth read it over and over again trying to make sense of it, the only thing that she couldn't truly comprehend was the verse about the jewellery box as she only knew about that in her dream. She even told Laura about it and described the contents before she had even opened it, as if she actually visited by her mother in her dream.

Ruth thought about the time that she was asked by Fiona from Criminal World magazine to help with investigations in Scotland, she was involved with searching for cursed mirrors which brought her back to her present predicament temporarily, she was wondering where Pamela had gone. She soon thought back to other incidents where Pamela could have rescued her. It made her think, was Pamela a ghost or a guardian angel, which ever she was Ruth was grateful for her help. At the Harrington household she was in a bad situation with a reporter from Criminal World who was arguing with her when two of the mirrors came to life. Three mirrors existed and were said to be part of the Harrington Curse

Two of the three mirrors were placed in the library temporarily until they could be united with the other mirror in the study, but while they were sorting this out Samantha decided to enter the study looking for Fiona. Instead she saw Ruth sat at a table reading one of the many books out of the book cabinet.

"Where's Fiona?" she asked.

"I don't know," Ruth replied sensing hostility in Samantha's voice.

"No of course you don't," Samantha said sarcastically.

"What's that supposed to mean?" Ruth asked.

"Nothing, I mean you haven't tried to make a pass at her then?" Samantha said, "I mean she is pretty!"

"Look just because she's pretty it doesn't mean I am going to fancy her," Ruth said in her own defence.

"She's blonde like Pamela, but she's straight. Shame isn't it," Samantha said rudely.

"Look just because I am a lesbian it doesn't mean I like every beautiful woman!" Ruth said angrily. At that moment the mirror began to glow and blood poured down it. But Samantha and Ruth were that busy arguing they hadn't noticed any activity.

"Why have you got to knock gay people?" Ruth asked.

"It's you I don't like, my God you think you invented sex especially lesbianism,"

"I stand up for my own kind, what's wrong with that?" Ruth asked.

"No you flaunt it and throw it in people's faces, both you and Pamela did that on all those fashion shows," Samantha said in disgust.

"Just because it was on television and radio, we were hounded by the press," Ruth explained.

"Fucking exhibitionism if you ask me," Samantha said.

"Not at all, everyone was against us, we merely defended

ourselves, against religion and political extremists," Ruth replied. "We had to challenge them."

"No you didn't that's a lame excuse," Samantha said beginning to pace up and down.

"So you think the likes of priests are perfect, those who abuse young boys, they are so fucking untouchable, so righteous!" Ruth was getting angry.

"How can you say that?" Samantha asked.

"Why don't you read the papers or magazines?" Ruth said pointing to a newspaper on the table.

"I do they are inaccurate and lie to sell the papers," Samantha said folding her arms in defence.

"Like Criminal World, I mean you as a crime reporter?" Ruth was referring to all reporters not just Criminal World's staff.

"Just keep your lesbian ideas to yourself," Samantha said looking away from her.

"What are you afraid of?" Ruth asked.

"Nothing," Samantha replied swiftly.

"Yes you are that's why your against me, you're frightened of something, perhaps things that you don't know about," Ruth said realising that what Samantha was referring to ran deeper than she would care to admit.

"That's fucking rubbish," Samantha said refusing to give Ruth eye contact.

"I've touched a nerve haven't I Sammy?" Ruth said trying to

get her to look at her.

"No I am not gay or anything!" Samantha said in disgust.

"You don't attack someone for no reason, and you said you're not homophobic, so what is it?" Ruth said probing her.

"Fuck you!" Samantha said unable to answer properly.

"I will find out. I am not being hated for nothing, you must have a reason, and so what is it?" Ruth was determined to find out the truth.

"Okay you're right," she turned and looked at Ruth. "My sister committed suicide because she was a lesbian, her girlfriend and she had a fight and her friend left her. She said it was due to watching you and Pamela on television that convinced her that she was gay. She followed your story and when things went wrong she took her own life."

"I am sorry," Ruth said sincerely.

"No I am sorry, I blamed you but I can see now I was wrong," Samantha admitted.

At that moment the room shook and books started to fly in mid-air. They were both dodging the books and then noticed a snake slither out of the mirror. Ruth pushed Samantha to the floor as a series of poison darts flew in the air and pinned Ruth to the door. Samantha got up and managed to block a dart with a book as it was flying towards Ruth's head, then the snake travelled towards Samantha with its mouth wide open. At that moment Pamela appeared and grabbed the snake and threw it back into the mirror, but only Samantha saw Pamela who smiled at her before she vanished.

Ruth was helping the other people involved with the investigation of the cursed mirrors of Zyanya, she explains about what she has discovered and offers to help further by going with them to Mexico.

"It's all about cause and effect, we witnessed one thing, call it a mass hallucination if you like. The cause could have been some kind of chemical imbalance like the mirrors in the Harrington household that contained a drug powerful enough to cause hallucinations or something in the food or drink who knows!" Ruth said pausing for a reaction. "The cause was the drug and the reaction or effect was hallucinations, delusions and illusions, and mirrors playing mind games. The way I see it is we all need closure with this and the only way is to go to Mexico and destroy the mirrors, only then can we put an end to this business. As for the article we can offer various explanations and leave the reader to decide what caused all the misery, just a thought Fi," Ruth said looking around the room as everyone applauded.

"Nice one Ruth," Samantha said smiling.

Ruth often considered herself lucky to survive after years of abuse and it was not through self determination to keep going despite the flashbacks, night terrors and nightmares not to mention the other reminders of the experience like after shave, music and tone of voice. But when her younger sister decided to confide in her and explain about her own abuse that Ruth decided to do more about such abusers and began to campaign against such monsters. As Ruth rightly said why the hell should people get away with it? Looking back, she remembered the time when Claire told her about her experience, when she first discussed about being abused.

Claire was sat on a settee in the lounge; she appeared very insular, agitated and withdrawn. Ruth sat beside her and was quiet for a while, Claire was nervous and jumpy reluctant to converse with Ruth. Her bottom lip was a little scabby as if she had been biting it in an agitated moment just has she had done when biting her nails.

"Claire what's wrong?" Ruth said using the direct approach.

"Nothing," Claire replied.

"You can tell me I will understand," Ruth pleaded.

"Just leave me!" Claire shouted.

"Something is hurting you inside isn't it?" Ruth continued.

"No, no, no!" Claire repeated suddenly crying.

Ruth pulled her close to her and found it difficult to hold back the tears herself.

"My God, he abused you too," Ruth said beginning to cry realising exactly what had happened.

"He told me to say nothing or he would blame me, he also said I would have to go away like you did," Claire explained.

"So it was Dad. I knew it," Ruth said angrily.

"Yes it began after you left home," Claire said sadly.

"Well the bastards dead now, we have to move on," Ruth said stroking Claire's hair.

Diane was standing in the doorway joined by Emma, "When will it end, this family is cursed," she said bitterly.

"Take my pain away Ruth," Claire insisted.

"You hold on Claire we will fight this one together, I've survived this and so will you," Ruth looking into the eyes of another victim, it was like looking into a mirror at her own soul.

"We are all here for you Claire," Emma added.

"Whatever it takes we are close by to help you," Ruth said.

"Yes you have us close by we are supporting each other remember," Emma said stroking her arm and hugging her.

Ruth spent a lot of time with Claire encouraging her to talk to her and sharing the awful experience with her. She also took Claire for counselling and waited for her outside the room in case she needed her. Ruth became so close to Claire and fulfilled her promise in looking after her and protecting her from harm. Claire needed Ruth's strong personality to help her cope with her trauma; Ruth was ideal providing sisterly love and professional help. Claire was very grateful to Ruth, as she knew how much trouble Ruth had been in and what she had been through herself. She knew that with Ruth's help she would be stronger and able to move on, confident that she could survive her past history of abuse.

Ruth could only be patient and hope that Claire would make it through the session, without feeling too bad. Ruth wondered what it would be like for Claire to come out of her solitude of safety like she did. Coming into the light from the dark and lonely place although it was never clear whether or not she used the wardrobe as a hiding place like she did.

Ruth had been helped by so many people that it built up

her wavering faith in humanity, she was also responsible for helping others but she proved that you can only help others if you are strong enough mentally. People loved Ruth and proved it in the kindness that they showed her, she had good friends and family who really did care. Friends like Kathy, Sheena and Gloria who were with her when it mattered to guide her and comfort her through rough times. Ruth now had to face her present predicament believing that she was really dead and awaiting the next passage to wherever she was to go. At that moment Pamela returned and had brought with her their mother Sarah.

Sarah looked upon her daughter and wept, Ruth was astonished by the resemblance and could see the love in her eyes, and those large eyes seemed to speak volumes as she gazed upon Ruth just as she had dreamt of her.

"Ruth my child, how are you?" she asked embracing her.

"Mother I can't believe it's you standing before me," Ruth said.

"I am so sorry things have gone so wrong for you," Sarah said kissing her forehead and stroking her hair.

"It is like talking to me," Ruth said smiling.

"You should smile more often," Sarah commented.

"You were so brave dealing with MS and trying to survive after everything else," Ruth said.

"No my dear you're the brave one with the life that you have had," Sarah said looking across at Pamela. "Or should I say you both had."

"But you were raped and killed," Ruth said. "And what's more I lived with one of the men that attacked you and didn't even know!"

"How would you know?" Sarah asked.

"But I still feel bad," Ruth said crying.

"Hush Ruth please don't cry I don't blame you so don't blame yourself for my death or Pamela's," Sarah had a soft calm voice that made Ruth relax.

"I feel better now you're here," Ruth said allowing her mother to wipe the tears from her eyes.

"That's good you need to prepare yourself for your next journey," Sarah explained.

"Where is that, where am I going?" Ruth asked looking at Sarah and then Pamela.

"This is to be your transitions so I want you to be brave and face all your demons in order to move on," Sarah pointed to the door. "Go through there and walk along the passageway then you will reach a second door, but don't look back or try to re-enter the door that you left. You need to move forward on and on until you reach the light, this is the only way you will face your future. We will come to the door with you but as for the journey you face that alone, that way you will gain strength and understanding."

"But mother I am afraid," Ruth admitted.

"Please be brave for a while longer and think of us who have made the journey already."

"Well if I can face mirrors, masks and psychopaths I guess I can face anything."

"That's my girl, now stand and walk with us," Sarah said confidently.

Ruth stood up and walked with them to the door; once they were in the doorway both Sarah and Pamela embraced her and then vanished.

Ruth walked into the dark passage as she entered the door shut behind her, she looked back and tried to open the door but it was locked.

"Oh shit," Ruth said to herself.

Then began walking along nervously until she reached a chair, it had a rag doll on it wearing a porcelain mask. But Ruth brushed past it as if it didn't exist. Then she entered another door and aluminous masks were floating all around her each one looked familiar, but she brushed past them and moved on. She felt uneasy as she entered the next door, she could smell aftershave and body sweat. It was like entering a men's changing room, her heart began pounding in her chest so hard she thought it was about to burst. But still she walked on, she began to sweat and tremble.

"Is anybody there, don't fuck with my head," she said loudly.

But no one was there, so she entered the next door and to her surprise she saw Malcolm imprisoned behind a glass wall, he was sat crouched forward staring at the floor.

"Malcolm why are you here is this hell?" Ruth asked.

"Ruth let me out please, you can do this," he pleaded. "You

have put me here so you can free me."

"No, you have committed the worst crimes ever, rape murder and abuse, you will be here forever," Ruth shouted.

"But I'm so sorry and I will do well from now on," Malcolm pleaded.

"I don't trust you sorry," she said dismissively.

"Come on you bitch get me out before I break the glass!" he said angrily.

"You can sit there and fucking rot for all I care," Ruth replied scornfully.

Ruth moved on through the next door in the next room her father George sat with his arms folded

"Dad, why am I not surprised to see you here?" Ruth said.

"Ruth, at last you know I am innocent," George said eagerly.

"Are you serious?" Ruth said coldly.

"But I didn't know about Ron, he fooled me and I did beat him up when I found out," George seemed remorseful at first, but soon blamed Ruth.

"Why father?" Ruth asked.

"What?" George stood to his feet.

"Why lie to me, why punish me?" Ruth shouted.

"You are to blame not me, flaunting your body," George shouted back.

"I never did I was a child, a vulnerable child and you took

advantage of me and my sister, both Ron and you are monsters," Ruth said banging the glass

"No!" George banged back.

"Yes you ruined my life and Claire's you filthy animal, you can stay here and rot, you are the reason I have nightmares and self harm, you make me physically sick I hate every part of you!"

Ruth put her back to the glass and slid down, sitting on the floor and listening to her father shout and bang on the glass then Ruth walked casually to the next door, not even reacting to his threats and not looking back.

The next room was similar as she noticed a glass wall and behind it was Raven.

"Raven fancy meeting you again," Ruth said bravely.

"My pretty young mental health nurse, how are you?"

"No better for seeing you Raven," Ruth said abruptly.

"Be nice to me for I have found God and he tells me you are an angel," Raven said softly.

"You were one of the few people that I could say were mentally ill," Ruth said cheerily. "Schizophrenic and definitely psychotic!"

"Go screw yourself I am as sane as you," Raven shouted.

"Your tone explains everything, goodbye Raven," she said leaving the room. Raven continued to curse and swear at her.

When she entered the next room she felt a kind of sadness

which overwhelmed her as she walked toward the glass wall. Behind the glass stood Colin dressed like Ruth, he was sat looking at Ruth with a sad expression on his face. He represented Ruth's sadness and despair and that's why she responded as she did, her heart was open to him.

"My princess let me near you," Colin begged.

"I can't I am sorry, but you have killed people, women who did you no harm," Ruth explained.

"No," he shouted. "You are wrong I protected you!"

"You wanted to be me," Ruth said. "You said only one of us can exist."

"I died for you!" Colin screamed. "I am the killer queen!"

"No," Ruth shouted. "Don't bring me into it. I can't make excuses for what you did or justify why I let you die!"

"You destroyed me," Colin said wildly.

"Get the fuck out of my head, leave my life, my sad days are over," Ruth said and walked on to the next room.

In the next room Frank was hitting his head on the wall; Ruth stood by the wall and began to talk to him.

"Stop!" She shouted he slowed down and then sat on the floor, "My God, don't you think you of all people deserve to be here?"

"I know but you caused me harm and said I deserved to die," Frank replied.

"You have harassed and murdered my family what else can

I think?" Ruth said.

"Find it in your heart to forgive me and blame yourself for your family being murdered, you took me to them and murdered them. See the blood on your hands it's your mothers," Frank said smirking.

"I never did that I don't know where this blood is from, it may be mine," Ruth said.

"Your blood from your heart and you feel no pain," Frank said laughing.

"I bleed because I am human and I have feeling's that is the difference between us, I have a heart and feel love, you are an empty shell and are condemned to hell."

Frank fell to the floor with his arms and legs spread and shouted over and over again, "No!"

Ruth composed herself before entering the next room, unaware that this was the last room. But the most challenging as this one contained Ron her childhood abuser, he was pacing up and down his cell and making faces at her behind the glass. She was clearly nervous and her heart pounded, she began to perspire and felt faint. Before she was able to speak she began to vomit.

"Hello darling, have you come for more?" he said in a creepy voice.

"I blamed my father for you and I believe he beat you up," Ruth said calmly.

"He knew about me and let me carry on," Ron said coldly.

"People like you deserve all you get; the problem is most of you get away with it. You are vile despicable creatures the lowest form of life in a pond," Ruth said angrily.

"You people beg for it!" Ron shouted.

"You monster!" Ruth shouted. "Evil monster!"

"Don't you want to vomit again weak child?" Ron jested.

"No I don't because you have actually cured that part of me and I am whole again." Ruth said confidently.

"One day your kind will be punished and then justice will be done. Until then fuck off and suffer in this place alone," Ruth smiled and turned her back on him.

Ron just kept banging his head on the wall till he bled. Ruth heard his head banging and walked up to the door. As she opened the door a bright light shone into her face. She had reached her destination.

RECOVERY

Ruth held her arm up shielding her eyes, while her other arm was fastened to a board with a venflon in her arm with intravenous fluids flowing into her veins. She began to focus on the room and noticed a nurse by the side of her bed; she smiled at Ruth and spoke softly but with authority.

"Well it's about time you woke up Ruth," she said picking up a clip board and revealing an observation chart.

"I take it I am not dead then?" Ruth asked.

"No, you're very much alive judging from these observations," she showed Ruth.

"I'll take your word for it," Ruth said turning over in the bed.

"Excuse me what are you doing?" she asked.

"What?" Ruth asked in surprise.

"Why are you sleeping?" she said sternly.

"Wait, who are you again?" Ruth said turning back towards her.

"I am Alison your nurse," Alison said surprised at Ruth's attitude.

"Well Alison I am Ruth Ashley psychiatric nurse who is apparently very much alive, but tired and I want to go to fucking sleep so piss off!" Ruth said rudely.

"Well I have never been so insulted in all my life," Alison said a little amused at Ruth's manner.

"Well clearly you don't go to many places," Ruth said realising that Alison was finding her amusing.

"You were right about her Sheena she can be a handful," Alison said speaking to Sheena who was standing next to her.

"Hi Ruth how are you doing bitch!" Sheena said laughing.

"Sheena," Ruth said excitedly. "I am so pleased to see you."

"Hey and you're not dead you don't die young remember!" Sheena reminded Ruth about a comment she made once when she was modelling.

"I will never die young, I remember telling you that," Ruth laughed then realised how dry her throat was. "How long was I out?" she asked holding her throat.

"Days," Alison said frowning.

"Can I have a drink?" Ruth asked.

"Yes alright but sips only," Alison advised.

"Sips?" Ruth asked.

Sheena poured some water from a jug into a beaker and passed it to her, Ruth began shaking so Sheena steadied the beaker while Ruth took sips from it.

"See I can do as I am told Alison," she said giggling.

"Behave Ruth," Sheena said giggling with her.

"Now I need to piss!" Ruth said biting her lip.

"You don't mean that?" Sheena asked.

"Yes I haven't been for days," Ruth said wriggling.

"Yes you have," Alison said. "In your pad."

"Oh Christ!" Ruth said alarmed. "I pissed myself?"

"Sort of," Alison said amused.

"I am like an old woman with issues!" Ruth said devastated.

She was helped to the toilet but felt so dizzy she needed a wheelchair back to the bed. By this time Cheryl had arrived with flowers and fruit, she was surprised to see Ruth awake and ran over to greet her.

"Hello wife!" Cheryl said smiling. "Are you well?"

"Hi Cheryl darling are you well?" Ruth asked.

"Clearly you are," Cheryl replied. "Or you appear so!"

"Cheryl I am really feeling good better than ever," Ruth said holding her arms up.

"I am alive!"

"Good," Cheryl said surprised.

"No better than good, awesome!" Ruth said trying to emphasis the point.

"I'm pleased," Cheryl said louder.

"I mean all my demons have gone I faced them and destroyed them at last," Ruth announced.

"Full recovery then," Sheena said making light of the situation.

With that Fiona and Samantha appeared also with flowers, Fiona had a plaster on her forehead, but had a booming smile.

"Oh thank God you're awake," Fiona said with relief.

"Yes I have been here everyday haven't I Cheryl?" Samantha said nudging her with her elbow.

"I am overwhelmed," Ruth said looking at all the flowers. "There are a few empty gardens then!"

Ruth spent a few days in the hospital before returning back to Cheryl. Alison made a fuss of her before she left and even shed a tear. Ruth didn't realise how popular she was, it was as if she was in a cloud of despair and guilt over the deaths of so many people and now she was cleansed and freed from her burden. It took the trauma of her car accident to jolt her into reality; it was as if a heavy load had been lifted from her shoulders. Perhaps the curse of Zyanya had also brought her back to her senses and she was whole again. Her broken wings were mended and she was no longer a lost soul, she always used to listen to a song by Kate Bush and Peter Gabriel called 'don't give up' and she obviously remembered the lyrics.

When she was well enough she visited the graves of all those who had died such as Pamela, Sarah her real mother, Diane and Kathy, Pamela was standing beside her smiling, she was so glad that Ruth had finally resolved her issues.

Ruth felt as if she was there for a reason and not to just visit the graves, she noticed a woman the same age as her who had placed flowers on Kathy's grave. She had fair hair, a slim figure and a rather prominent chin.

"Rebecca Rogers!" Ruth said with surprise.

"Ruth Ashley!" she replied.

"What a surprise I haven't seen you for a while," Ruth said hugging her.

"I was at Kathy's funeral but I had to leave in a hurry my daughter was ill," she explained.

"You have a daughter?" Ruth asked a little puzzled.

"Yes I went through the gay thing but I guess it was a fad, who knows," she said looking back at the grave. "I should have kept in touch with Kathy; she was my mentor when I was a student nurse, that was when you were in the community as a student nurse and when you were dating that psycho."

"She was my best friend and helped me a lot," Ruth said also looking at her grave.

"So are you still with that psycho?" Rebecca asked.

"Who do you mean Malcolm?" Ruth asked.

"How many psycho boyfriends have you had, yes Malcolm!" Rebecca said frowning.

"God no, he died thank goodness," Ruth seemed puzzled. "Haven't you heard on TV, the papers or anything?"

"No I have been nursing abroad," Rebecca said. "But I had Lauren and then divorced the waste of space and left him in Greece," Rebecca continued.

"So what will you do now?" Ruth said inquisitively.

"Get a job back here I suppose," Rebecca said with a smile on her face

"You have got a job haven't you?" Ruth asked anticipating the answer.

"Yes on your ward!" Rebecca seemed so excited.

"Becky, no way really, that's great!" Ruth was equally excited. "Students together now nursing together, how exciting!"

"Yes we had fun, listen Ruth I have to go but we will no doubt catch up okay?" She said taking a last look at Kathy's grave.

"Sure see you soon" Ruth said watching her walk away.

Ruth resumed her counselling sessions but had a new counsellor to contend with, Janet had taken over from her previous counsellors and so she had to build up a therapeutic relationship with her just as she had with the others. But Janet was experienced in life and had been affected by abuse and could empathize with Ruth, this made it easier for her to understand. A previous counsellor called Sheila had explained a few things to Janet so that she could be prepared for her, she had a vomit bowl in place with tissues, the window was open making the room airy, and she also provided Ruth with a jug of water and a fresh shiny beaker. Ruth noticed an absence of magazines that might contain masks or other items to upset her, in fact a lot of thought had gone into making the environment suitable for Ruth. Janet gestured Ruth to sit down on an easy chair, she ensured that

Ruth was comfortable before she began to talk to her.

"Hi my name is Janet I am your counsellor," she said introducing herself.

"Well to begin with I like the atmosphere," Ruth said spreading her arms out in an open gesture as if she was performing like Kate Bush. "It's comfortable and airy," she said as if she was acting out the song Wuthering Heights.

"Okay that's good," Janet said with surprise

"Oh, but you can lose the vomit bowl I won't be using that, you evidently heard about me vomiting in the rubbish bin!" Ruth said jokingly. "That is unless you want it?"

Janet looked a little embarrassed by Ruth's remark, surprised by her direct approach. She expected a woman with anxiety and in a highly volatile situation, shouting, becoming tearful and vomiting as Sheila had described her.

"To be honest I am so surprised that you are so relaxed," Janet admitted.

"Yes I suppose that I am a new woman with complex needs," Ruth said. "And so this is where we build up a therapeutic relationship, we get to know each other and I tell you my most intimate secrets and you try not to be judgmental even though I am a raving lesbian!"

"Well Ruth that's quite intense and tells me that you have knowledge of counselling," Janet said. "So what do you want to get out of this session?"

"Well for a start don't use sentences like how does that make you feel," Ruth explained. "It's so annoying and text book."

"So that's one ground rule so far," Janet said taking notes. "And with no abusive behaviour or swearing!"

"I am joking," Ruth said. "So you don't really know me!" "Sheila did say that you are a remarkable woman but that's as much as I can say about what we discussed," Janet said watching Ruth's reaction.

"Did she mention the ghost or a strange experience?" Ruth asked.

"No comment," Janet said looking around the room.

"Don't worry she won't appear unless I am being threatened," Ruth said smiling.

"Then let's make sure that it doesn't happen," Janet said smiling back.

Janet was a fifty-year-old woman who was slim with a long thin nose her dark hair was fairly short with brown highlights.

"So where would you like to begin?" Janet asked.

"Well, can I tell you about when I was in a coma experiencing something, maybe an epiphany or something?" Ruth said.

"Yes alight" Janet agreed.

"I may have died after being in a car crash and met ghosts from my past, the first ones where family and friends, but then I met my abusers, Malcolm, Ron and others." Ruth said.

"And how did that make you feel?" Janet said before realising what she said.

"So cliché Janet really," Ruth said.

"Sorry Ruth it slipped out, carry on," Janet admitted.

"Well I felt exhilarated at the sight of my family, but like shit when the abusers appeared, they fucked with my head big time!" Ruth admitted.

"Malcolm was my ex boyfriend who at first appeared kind and considerate, he was polite with me but tended to be rude to other people. I realised that it was all a show for me as he began to get abusive towards me," Ruth explained.

"Why what did he do?" Janet said seeming to understand exactly what Ruth was going through.

"He began by criticising me, verbally humiliating and taunting me, and then he became physical by slapping and kicking me. He was a control freak; he began by checking where I was going and even following me, as if I was having an affair with someone when in reality he was having affairs and visiting prostitutes. He even started throwing my meals up the wall or in the bin. He tried humiliating me by saying I was horrible and my body was out of proportion, I began believing him and becoming paranoid about certain things," Ruth was watching Janet's reactions.

"I should imagine you must have felt awful at this time?" Janet said.   "I did and the thought of him going with prostitutes made me feel dirty and then when he raped me," Ruth paused. "I thought he had passed on diseases."

"How awful," Janet said struggling to find the right things to say.

"I began to think it was me, that I was at fault just like when

Ron abused me, I felt that I had caused them to abuse me, that I encouraged them somehow by dressing tartly or made myself cheap in some way. I was also angry with myself for allowing it to happen, I just wanted to die at that time, and my life seemed worthless. Fortunately, I had Kathy who was a tower of strength, my rock."

Ruth seems a little tearful her voice became weak and quivery.

"Who is Kathy?" Janet asked.

"My dear friend and colleague who passed away," Ruth said. "I never really told her how much I appreciated her."

"I am sure she knew, she sounds like a nice lady," Janet said.

"She was," Ruth said feeling tears trickling from her eyes. "I loved her like my mother."

"Is your mother dead too?" Janet asked anticipating the answer.

"Yes she is," Ruth replied.

"What was her name?" Janet asked glancing at the clock discretely.

"My real mother was called Sarah," Ruth said. "Also I had a step mother called Diane."

"Malcolm killed my mother, I didn't know about this till after I left Malcolm he raped her and beat her to death, long before I met him. I hardly knew my mother I met her recently in a kind of dream, she had M.S she and my step sister Pamela lived together. Pamela was a model so pretty like a porcelain doll, then she was abused and in my mother's eyes became cracked porcelain." Ruth explained.

"Cracked porcelain?" Janet said on reflection. "You have all had a rough time."

"Suppose so and I suppose those who are abused are all cracked porcelain," Ruth replied.

"You have done well to get through things, so brave and unbelievably strong mentally," Janet said.

"I was weak but now I am gathering strength, I felt once that I had that experience of going through a door down a long corridor and entering a room with a glass panel separating me from my abusers, I told them what I thought of them, I could face anything!"

"Was it like a prison?" Janet asked.

"Yes with so many rooms each containing one of my abusers or enemies, I spoke to each in turn. But was it a dream or did I die and came back to life?" Ruth asked.

"I can't answer that, who knows its one of life's mystery's that we will find out about one day," Janet said. "But who knows one day all questions will be answered, it is however commendable that you got through things and fathomed out the answers to your questions."

"Thank you I have the feeling I do know the answer, but I am afraid to believe it," Ruth said.

The session ended and Ruth left the room believing that ghosts did exist, she entered the next session discussing each of Malcolm's brother Frank and Raven, the third session she discussed Colin. Ruth was injured by Malcolm, Frank, Raven and Colin. Raven was schizophrenic and so in Ruth's eyes she was mentally ill. But when Ruth discussed Colin on the fourth session and seemed to upset Janet by discussing mixed gender and transsexuals, it was as if she was aware of this from personnel experience.

"So was Colin a transvestite? Janet asked.

"Yes but he was one step further as he really wanted to be me," she looked at Janet. "He was like an impersonator, copying my mannerisms, dressing like me and said that he actually wanted to be me, but couldn't. So one of us had to die and as I am here, he is dead," Ruth glanced at Janet. "He murdered people who upset me, because if they upset me, he made out that he was obsessed with me and eventually killed himself."

"How did you feel about that?" Janet asked.

"It fucking freaked me out to be honest," Ruth admitted.

"Yes it sounds creepy to me and was he in that prison you mentioned?" Janet asked.

"Yes he was, he made me feel threatened, Malcolm made me feel humiliated, Frank was just a tosser and Raven was scary because of her interest in knives, my father got Ron involved in the family and we called him uncle Ron he was my first abuser from childhood," Ruth was trying to discuss everything at once and confused Janet.

"Let's stop there and continue next week," she said.

The following week Ruth discussed Ron and what he did in graphic detail, she even made Janet feel sick and she became tearful.

"It happened to you too didn't it?" Ruth asked.

"I can't say," Janet said.

"I know it did and that's why you reacted the way you did, I do understand I am a mental health nurse, trained to observe and recognise the signs," Ruth said stressing her role as a nurse.

"Yes I had a bad childhood that's why I help others," Janet said reluctantly.

"I am so sorry and you should have stopped me discussing it," Ruth said.

"It is a little freaky hearing someone else saying these things," Janet said.

"Men are real bastards, they think of us as sex toys or objects and not women, I know a handful of good men who are genuine that doesn't include my father George, but does include Geoff my psychiatric boss."

"So how are you now?" Janet asked.

"Getting stronger mentally, physically active, running the Race for Life later this year and getting involved in demonstrations to fight abuse. I also get involved in Manchester pride joining in the carnival procession and getting pissed," Ruth said.

"Good for you," Janet said.

"I still relive the car crash that led to my coma or sleep, everything in slow motion, walking into the light that is described in books and television in such things as ghost whisperer. Meeting the ghosts of friends and then visiting the prison as you describe it, speaking to my abusers and telling them what I think of them," Ruth continued. "It feels like a giant weight lifted off my shoulders telling you all about it and having met them abusers as an equal."

"I should imagine you do feel better," Janet said.

"And the fact that my younger sister was affected as well," Ruth said. "Claire was the next in line after me and they ruined her life too."

The session came to an end and Ruth sat down for a while her head was empty after off loading all her experiences, she had ten more sessions before she was happy to continue life without counselling. She discovered the answers that she was seeking regarding her dreams that she was strong enough to face her past and deal with issues rationally. She had put her ghost at rest or returned her demons to hell where they belong, hopefully never to return again. One strange thing happened in a dream, she saw a woman who looked like Ruth only she was older and had many problems. Ruth was confused about this woman and needed to know just who she was, looking rationally could it really be her and if so why was she in her dream. Was she there to warn Ruth about her future so that she could adjust her life or was this some other kind of message?

A GLIMPES OF THE FUTURE

Ruth continued to have dreams but not the night terrors or dreadful nightmares that she had formally experienced, where she would wake up with scratches on her body or other types of self harm.

She experienced something strange in a dream once where she was on the psychiatric ward nursing an older woman who had clinical depression. She was known to the system, typical revolving door case, with repeated admissions treating her psychosis. But Ruth felt that she resembled her but in her own future, she was timid and presented with episodes of paranoia constantly looking around her and feeling insecure.

But Ruth felt after her experience in the car crash and what followed that she was stronger and less likely to fall back into this state. Her life had improved and no one would come along to spoil things such as Malcolm, Frank, Raven or Colin. Even her childhood abuser was out of the equation following a tragic accident that cut short his life of abusing others. Visiting each of her attackers in that imaginary world in her mind seemed to help her to come to terms with her past, it also resolved issues of guilt on her behalf and gave her closure. But the situation like this dream seemed so real as if she was actually this woman and that she was nursing her through her depression. It made Ruth realise just how many people suffer in their own mind and some never completely share their thoughts, they live with unresolved issues and try to cope on a day to day basis. Sad faces of the poor victims of abuse, rape or other traumas, the things that they carry inside them and are too afraid to let them out. The monsters that rape the very soul from others and leave an empty shell, like cracked porcelain which Pamela and Ruth could relate to so clearly. The abuser goes free while the victim relives the experience over and over in their mind until they can no longer bear it. Not many truly recover from their mental torture, physically they heal but mentally they are scarred for life and experience nightmares, panic attacks and other equally nasty effects from such horrible memories.

Ruth looked on as the woman had electrical convulsive therapy (ECT) her body shaking like a person having a bad seizure. Then the woman is sat on the ward looking out of the window or appearing to do so, what must she be thinking, perhaps about her life in the outside world living amongst those more fortunate than themselves who have a family, a job and a circle of friends who care about them?

Ruth had her family and her friends that survived the many problems that faced them and they became stronger as a unit because of their love for each other. This was Ruth's understanding of her own past and why she was determined to be strong and think positively no matter what life threw at her. She was Ruth the mental health nurse who cared and saw the problems with others during their struggle to get well. People recognise these fine qualities in Ruth and never gave up on her, so she thought 'why should she give up on others'. Her philosophy in life centred on her own beliefs which were to help others as much as possible despite their condition, she believed in going that extra mile or give more than others think necessary.

Ruth awoke refreshed and with the thought of that patient in her mind, she walked into the shower and began to sing as she washed herself. Strangely enough she was singing a Kate Bush song called 'don't give up' which was a particular favourite of hers. Although she struggled with the high notes and changed to a less challenging song such as the 'power of love' by Frankie goes to Hollywood, but she preferred the Gabriel Aplin version that suited her voice. Cheryl was lying in bed and put the pillow over her ears curling up in a foetal position and groaning heavily until Ruth stopped.

"God Ruth, must you sing in the morning it's so annoying!" Cheryl said emerging from the pillow.

"Cheryl darling you really must be more cheerful," Ruth said throwing her towel at her and hitting her in the face.

"Piss off Ruth!" she said throwing the towel back at her and watching Ruth walking around naked. "God, you have a lovely body."

"Yes I have haven't I," Ruth said standing naked looking into the mirror.

"But then so have you."

"I think my tits are my best feature," Cheryl said opening the top to her pyjamas and revealing her breasts.

"Oh definitely and stop turning me on before I go to work," Ruth said laughing.

Ruth grabbed one of Cheryl's breasts and caressed it; she then kissed her on the lips and walked away as Cheryl slapped her on the behind.

"Love you Ruth," she said in a matter of fact manner.

"Love you more," Ruth replied.

Ruth was soon dressed and applied a little make up before heading towards the door.

"Oh remember it's your turn to get dinner ready," Ruth said turning to face her.

"Oh that would be beans on toast then," Cheryl added.

"Yeah right, like that's gonna happen!" Ruth joked.

"Okay, chilli, curry or spaghetti?" Cheryl reeled off ideas as Ruth opened the door and left.

Ruth popped her head back round the corner. "Whatever!"

When Ruth was driving to work she went down the street where Kathy once lived, she stopped by her place and looked towards the door almost expecting her to come out and jump into the car. She thought about the jolly smiling face and happy greeting from her friend. Sometimes the sarcastic remark because Ruth was late or smelt of garlic, but Kathy never mentioned her family not even to Ruth. She was aware of Ruth's situation and family life and didn't want to burden her not even about her cancer.

When she arrived at work Rebecca was already there and eager to start, the night staff handed over to the day staff informing them of the events of the night and any relevant information about the patients that needed to be passed forward.

Ruth wanted to discuss her experiences with Rebecca but

although they were students together she was reluctant to disclose anything until she had been with her for a while. If only Kathy was with her she would have been happy to listen and no doubt comment on what she heard, she wanted to reveal the entire epiphany. But that would be quite a feat especially as she though that Ruth was still with the 'psycho' Malcolm. Instead Ruth remained fairly quiet only discussing work and patient care.

But thought to herself, you can't move on until you let go she had read this once and took it on board once she recovered.

Ruth returned on the ward and focused on the patients and their needs, she was feeling particularly good. During the course of the day she met Elizabeth Shepherd a seventy-year-old patient who was suffering from chronic depression. She was so bad that she could hardly express her needs and would scream and shout at times, and then have long periods of silence. She was very thin and refused food, clenching her lips and spitting, sometimes she would put her fingers down her throat and vomit. Ruth was disturbed by this but what upset her more is that she reminded her of the dream she had because the woman looked exactly like her. She wondered whether her presence had some significance of her own future, was her dream a prophecy or a warning.

Ruth tried to clear the thoughts from her mind and proceeded to walk around the ward observing the patients and staff. Rebecca was also on the ward getting to know everyone and settling in to her new environment just as Ruth once did. She appeared to be watching Ruth which at times made Ruth feel uneasy as she wasn't used to this, not since Kathy had died. It was almost as if Kathy had returned as mother hen watching over her chicks, Rebecca was not conscious of watching Ruth or appeared not to be, but Kathy had in fact asked her to support Ruth. Rebecca had only told Ruth what she wanted to hear and never mentioned that Kathy had contacted her about Ruth months before her death.

Kathy was clever and able to foresee Ruth's life after her death and that she needed someone strong to be beside her at work, someone who would guide and protect her as Kathy had done. Like a bright star or glowing lantern Rebecca was the light that shone for Ruth in Kathy's absence, Rebecca was sensible and mature for her age.

Rebecca was the main nurse to care for Elizabeth who ensured she was washed and dressed, took her medication and other treatment. Including Electrical convulsive therapy (ECT) which was an effective treatment, but awful to watch people being treated as they experienced electricity being charged through their body. The body convulses like somebody experiencing a seizure and then it's over, they say some people lose part of their memory but that's questionable. Ruth was present when Elizabeth was having her treatment and her expression seemed to tell the story of events as Ruth expressed every moment with her eyes. It was as if Ruth was relaying her entire past in a few moments, each jerk was one of Ruth's tragic moments glimpsed and gone. After the treatment Elizabeth was taken out on a stretcher and Rebecca held Ruth's arm as if to tell her that she knew and understood. It was at that moment that Ruth realised that Kathy had mentioned her and asked her to watch over her. Ruth smiled and shed a tear at that precise time Ruth felt good and she could actually feel Kathy's presence.

Ruth returned to the ward focused on her work with the patients she referred to as her people with broken wings and lost souls, she felt good having fathomed out her past with the help from her new counsellor Janet. Ruth thought about the new patient Elizabeth and how much of her past resembled her own, her history of abuse and the depression, even her features were similar. Rebecca could see that Ruth was troubled and offered to comfort her, she hugged her but Ruth was used to being comforted by Kathy and felt a little uncomfortable with Rebecca.

"Ruth, I knew about you at the graveside, about Malcolm and Pamela, but I said nothing," Rebecca admitted. "Kathy just told me so that I could help you."

"I know I didn't want to discuss it anyway," Ruth replied.

"But you seem troubled now?" Rebecca said concerned.

"No, I just see myself in Elizabeth, like part of my past, present and future," Ruth bowed her head.

"You are not like her, she is severely damaged by her past and the process is irreversible," Rebecca explained. "Go and meet her, find out for yourself."

Ruth walked up to Elizabeth and smiled "Hi Elizabeth my name is Ruth may I join you?"

"Yes if you want, sit beside me and call me Beth," Elizabeth said.

"Okay Beth, nice to meet you," Ruth said trying to look in her eyes.

"I know who you are," Elizabeth replied to Ruth's surprise.

"I don't understand," Ruth said confused.

"I know who you are and why you are here," Elizabeth continued. "How is Pamela?"

"She passed away," Ruth replied.

"I know but she exists in the spirited realm," Elizabeth sounded very eyrie.

"How do you know that?" Ruth asked nervously.

"I know all about you Ruth," she continued almost in a trance.

"Do you know me?" Ruth asked. "Or has someone mentioned me?"

"You are a poor, tragic child," she muttered.

"But where do you know me from?" Ruth asked.

"I am aware of your life with Malcolm, Pamela and Cheryl."

"I really don't understand," Ruth was becoming quite anxious in her presence.

"You will understand eventually," Elizabeth touched Ruth's hand. "Now let me rest," she said waving her hand to dismiss her.

Ruth tried to question her further but she closed her eyes and turned away. When Ruth caught up with Rebecca she explained the conversation to her discussing every detail.

"My God Ruth that sounds a bit weird," Rebecca said.

"Well, she obviously knows me somehow," Ruth said. "I

remember dreaming about her a while ago."

"Really," Rebecca said surprised.

"Perhaps on reflection you should avoid her for a while, meeting her might have been a mistake," Rebecca said concerned.

"She said in the dream that love would save us," Ruth said.

"How odd and what does that mean?" Rebecca asked.

"Fuck knows but it sounds odd and she was definitely strange," Ruth said shrugging her shoulders. "I heard it a long time ago I did feel it was apt with my lifestyle."

"A bold statement," Rebecca said.

"Yes I thought so," Ruth said.

Later Rebecca was talking to Elizabeth and she mentioned Ruth speaking as if she knew her.

"Look after the nurse with the broken wings and lost souls," she said.

"Who do you mean?" Rebecca asked already anticipating the answer.

"Why Ruth Ashley of course!"

"Why is she hurt?" Rebecca asked.

"Yes inside she bares the scars and some externally, but she can repair herself unlike me, tell her love will save us," she said leaving Rebecca shocked.

"How did you know that statement?" Rebecca asked.

"It is written on all of our hearts and comes to us in our dreams," she said looking at Rebecca. "Sarah used to quote it."

"Sarah?"

"Ruth's mother," she said smiling.

"But she was Diane," Rebecca said confused.

"Her real mother Sarah, Pamela's mother," she said closing her eyes.

"You knew Sarah?" Rebecca said frowning.

"I know Sarah," she said waving her hand to dismiss Rebecca.

Rebecca stood up and felt Elizabeth grabbing her hand, but her eyes remained closed. "Tell Ruth Sarah watches over her as Pamela does and not to be afraid of anything."

Elizabeth released her grip and for a while Rebecca's hand felt cold, she went into the office where Ruth was sat writing reports and stood in silence. It was as if some strange phenomenon had occurred and Rebecca was trying to fathom it out in her mind. But nothing seemed to make sense as Elizabeth seemed to be speaking about Sarah not in the past tense but as if she were still alive and in contact with her like a medium or clairvoyant. She took her file from the desk where Ruth had been reading it and sat reading it herself.

"You won't find much in there," Ruth said.

"Really, because I have had the strangest conversation with her about you," Rebecca said.

"Was it about my mother?" Ruth asked.

"Yes how did you know?" Rebecca said baffled.

"I guessed by our conversation, Beth knew Sarah my real mother didn't she?" Ruth seemed calmer.

"She actually said that she knows your mother," Rebecca replied.

At that moment there was a lot of rushing about and people were running into Elizabeth's room, seeing the activity both Ruth and Rebecca ran out of the office and into the corridor. Ruth entered the door first seeing staff trying to resuscitate Elizabeth.

"Did she speak to anyone?" Ruth asked.

"No one," a medic replied.

At that moment she opened her eyes and stared at Ruth, looking into her eyes and smiling. "Love will save us," she said then faded away.

The colour in Ruth's face drained and she collapsed, Rebecca ran towards her and yelled, "Ruth!" she knelt by her side and addressed a doctor. "Is she dead too?"

"No she has just fainted," he said.

"But she is very weak and obviously she was traumatised by this experience," he replied.

"This is so unlike Ruth she is usually so strong and handles situations like this all the time!" Rebecca commented.

Ruth soon came round and seemed bewildered by all the

activity around her.

"What's going on?" she muttered. "Wait, has Beth died?"

"Yes Ruth," Rebecca said holding her shoulder.

Ruth had been taken outside the room and placed on a settee Rebecca had remained with her. Ruth stood with support from Rebecca and another member of staff.

"I want to see her," Ruth insisted.

"But Ruth do you think you should?" Rebecca asked.

"Don't even try to stop me Becky," Ruth gave Rebecca the type of look that warned her to steer clear of her at this time.

Ruth glanced in Elizabeth's room and noticed her lying so peacefully like a porcelain doll, so calm so still appearing to have no worries. Her body was so relaxed evidently free from the problems of the world, which was a nice place to be no matter what anybody believed in, death brought about peace and the end of suffering.

ACTS OF KINDNESS

Princess Diane once said 'Carry out a random act of kindness with no expectation of reward, safe in the knowledge that one day someone might do the same for you'

It was a warm summer's morning everything was calm and still, the trees in the park were in full bloom and most people were having a morning stroll down the pathways alone, with dogs or as a couple. But four female figures were jogging along keeping fit and determined to reach their destination with a purpose in mind. It was time for the Race for Life and to raise money for Cancer Research, such dedicated people often ran through this park covering a circuit of four to five miles a day. The more experienced runners managed more and would race each year spending many hours training before the big event. Ruth led her faithful team in such an event explaining that running was good for their mental well-being as well as physical health.

Suddenly the runners stopped and rested on a grass verge, each one lay down in turn exhausted.

"Come on girls why have you all stopped we have miles to go," Ruth said jogging on the spot.

"Ruth we are beat let's rest," Sheena said puffing and panting.

"Yes Ruth stop being a task master!" Gloria agreed.

"Come on Cheryl one more lap," Ruth insisted.

"Ruth that's enough really," Cheryl said resting her head on her knees.

"Come on Cheryl please," Ruth pleaded.

"Okay Ruth one more and that's it!" Cheryl agreed.

"Yay good stuff, we will meet you back here okay," Ruth said to Sheena and Gloria.

Ruth and Cheryl set off down the winding pathway around the park, Ruth wanted to break into a run but Cheryl was happy to jog along at a steady pace.

They were happy to just jog and not hold a conversation until they reached the tree where Raven died. Ruth stopped beneath the tree and took a breath.

"Are you okay Ruth?" Cheryl asked concerned.

"Yes of course," Ruth replied. "Just burying the past," Ruth said touching the tree.

"Oh okay," Cheryl replied.

"This was the tree that saved my life when Raven and I fought," Ruth explained. "She would have beat me too if I hadn't been rescued by someone."

"Yes Ruth I remember," Cheryl said.

"Okay let's go," Ruth said jogging on.

"You're very brave Ruth," Cheryl said stopping again.

"Nonsense Cheryl I'm only like everyone else, "she said patting Cheryl on the back.

"No Ruth you're special," Cheryl said kissing her on the lips.

"Thank you so are you, you're a brilliant artist," Ruth said smiling.

They continued to jog and eventually joined Sheena and Gloria who were still lying on the grass. They both sat up at the same time and seemed pleased to see Ruth and Cheryl as they ran towards them.

"Oh you decided to stay here then?" Ruth remarked. "Relaxing while we race for life!"

"Sorry Ruth we're knackered!" Sheena said laughing.

"We are not as fit as you Ruth," Gloria said laughing with Sheena.

"Okay but don't let me down on the day!" Ruth said.

"Okay we will be there," Sheena agreed.

"Yeah honestly Ruth we will be there we won't let you down," Gloria said confidently.

"Let's do it for cancer!" Cheryl said.

At that moment a police car passed by with its sirens blaring which made them jump. Ruth seemed to respond the worst.

"Don't you just love Manchester it's so lively!" Ruth said.

"Well I suppose it's the same in any city," Sheena replied.

"Well, see you tomorrow girls," Ruth continued. "Here again?"

"No problem," Sheena said walking away with Gloria.

They trained for a few months and finally the event took place, Ruth was pleased with the turn out and with the efforts made by Cheryl and her friends. The race for Life raised a lot of money for Cancer Research, but Ruth was not content with doing this and organised a demonstration in London and New York against abuse. She had a good team who were victims of abuse some with good leadership skills, who organised great crowds of people around Hyde park in London with live rock bands and banners stating the need for governments to clamp down on abuse and provide justice for the victims who suffer the affects for the rest of their lives. This was mirrored or repeated in New York in Central Park. Massive crowds emerged in support of this cause and it was compared with many previous demonstrations in size. The events were televised and broadcast all over the world; it was a peaceful demonstration that raised money to support the victims in many ways. Ruth tried to avoid exposure and simply wanted to blend into the background, but her fellow campaigners wouldn't allow this and pushed her to the foreground. Ruth never wanted fame, this reminded her of her brief modelling career which she hated, and she was not the type of woman who liked to be noticed or recognised as an extrovert or a seeker of fame. Often people misunderstood her intentions of becoming a model, she only did this to please Pamela, and she didn't even think she was all that attractive, but everyone considered her as beautiful with a slim shapely figure. She had the kind of looks that appealed to the eyes of men and women alike and often made people stare at her in the street which unnerved her.

The demonstration in New York began with people walking down many side walks with banners coming from various directions, being televised from above and across the streets by cameras. People were coming from other parts of New York City such as Brooklyn, Queens and the Bronx all determined to show their support to fight against abuse. They would meet in Central Park and then the guest speakers would express their opinions on abuse and speak for the many victims in the countries around the world. The rock concert also brought in the crowd with spectacular performances with guest bands and solo artists some who had written songs especially for the event.

Claire, Ruth's younger sister joined her in New York and they spent time alone after the demonstration, they were travelling around the city shopping in places such as Bloomingdales and Maces for clothes.

At one point they stood at the top of the Empire State Building and looked out at the breathtaking views such as Central Park.

"This is amazing," Claire said looking through the protective bars on one of the four sides of the observation area of the building.

Ruth's hair was blowing in the wind, but Claire had just had her hair shortened and so didn't experience this like Ruth or some of the other women standing there.

"I hate heights, but I love it up here it's one of the best views of New York," Ruth said taking a deep breath.

"I could live here," Claire said.

"Why don't you?" Ruth asked.

"I don't know I suppose I could work over here," Claire said.

"I'm free and single and I could get work here."

"Whatever makes you happy Claire," Ruth replied smiling.

Claire noticed a female security guard. "She's nice!"

"Claire," Ruth said pulling her round the corner.

"Well I can look can't I?" Claire said giggling. "I could be a security guard!"

"You could," Ruth agreed. "But why a security guard?"

"I like the uniform," Claire replied.

"You're mad," Ruth said touching her head with her finger. "Lots of jobs have uniforms."

"I guess so, police, fire service, army or traffic warden," Claire said thinking of more.

"Meter maid what kind of job is that annoying drivers and dishing out tickets," Ruth said watching Claire's reaction.

"I'm a traffic warden in Manchester!" Claire replied.

"So you are!" Ruth said laughing. "My little sister a meter maid!"

"My sister, who is a mental health nurse with issues!" Claire said laughing back. "And Emma our other sister who is a single mom."

"Is she?" Ruth asked.

"Yes that dopey half wit left her," Claire said. "He couldn't handle responsibility."

"She is better off without him, he was a loser," Ruth said

opening the door to go inside. "Let's get a drink."

"A diet coke for me Ruth," Claire said walking into the souvenir shop.

"We are here," Ruth said picking up an ornament of the Empire State Building and pointing to the top.

"King Kong," Claire said holding up a Gorilla climbing up the Empire State Building.

"Shall we go to Central Park for a picnic?" Claire suggested.

"Yes that would be nice," Ruth agreed.

They left the building and went into a store to pick up sandwiches and drinks, then hailed a yellow cab to take them to Central Park. It all seemed quiet after they had spent the previous day involved in the demonstration and rock concert. They jumped on a horse drawn carriage and travelled through the park, both pointing out various landmarks and attractive water features. They walked around and Claire continued to point out objects and statues. Claire was particularly interested in the Alice in wonderland statue with all the main characters such as the mad hatter and rabbit.

"I love that story," Claire said excitedly.

"The writer Lewis Carol was quite strange and as mad as his characters I think," Ruth said looking at Alice with the characters at her feet.

"Shall we find the carousel ride, I love roundabouts?"

"Yes alright," Ruth agreed.

"You did a good speech here Ruth, I cried when I heard what

you said about abuse and fighting the system in order to protect children and women from abuse," Claire said with admiration.

"Thank you sister," Ruth said. "I was thinking about us and our experience."

"Yes but we survived to tell the tale, some poor victims never did," Claire said. "Some committed suicide because they couldn't live with that kind of shit in their head."

"Yes and others went mad trying to live with it," Ruth explained. "It's the coping that is hard isn't it?"

"Yes you're right Ruth, I would never have made it without you," Claire admitted. "You're my rock," she said hugging Ruth.

"Hey Claire, you're my sister that's what sisters do," Ruth said kissing her on the forehead. "Now let's change the subject."

The next big event was Manchester pride which Ruth attended with friends every year, she joins transgender and transvestite friends dressed up in various costumes walking in the carnival and then entering the pubs in the gay community on Canal Street. As usual it was well turned out and a lively event with no problems, everyone was happy and free to do what they wanted without criticism. The whole idea was for everyone to have fun and not feel that they had to conform to a heterosexual world, they could freely express their sexuality. Gay pride was a worldwide thing introduced for the benefit of gay people and as a way of saying we exist and want the world to know and respect us. This is the message they are telling people and sharing the hope for the future that everyone can get on despite race, ethnicity and sexuality. Freedom is all about feeling as if you belong and being accepted for who and what you are and not what society dictates to suit them.

Ruth often mingled in the crowd and felt safe and secure in this environment, as opposed to a crowd in a busy airport or railway station. She is often suspicious of people who would sweep past her in a crowd, wondering whether or not they were paedophile, rapists or sociopaths at the least undesirable creeps as she would call them. In Ruth's eyes people had harmed her and some she thought she could trust, these people had affected her life so badly that the very thought of walking through crowds made her physically sick and she was prone to panic attacks where she would experience palpitations and became breathless. The only way of coping was to find a clear area and stand for a while and breathe, hoping that no one noticed her experiencing such an attack and trying to help her as they would often crowd her and make her worse. Being trapped in shops was a problem too as this made her feel like there was no way out and she would panic and perspire. This would take her back to her wardrobe experience the dark and secluded place where she hoped her abuser would never find her. But where would you find such a place in a station or in a store, Ruth used changing rooms and toilet cubicles.

Ruth considered that helping others was also helping herself and so she would think of her own anxieties and how she copes and helped others accordingly. This is what made Ruth special and people felt comfortable in her presence, she is considered lovable, kind and compassionate. An English rose in full bloom so beautiful with a healthy body that she cares for with her healthy diet and lotions.

Ruth is the type of person that you can confide in and share your thoughts without others knowing your secret; she lives to love and loves to live. This is why she helps with Manchester pride not just because she is a lesbian but because she genuinely cares for people.

Even with Ruth's philosophy of each to their own, she has no time for religion and considers that religion is one of the main causes of war. She feels that religion leads to misery and sorrow and that there is no happiness in believing in a God that allows cruelty and abuse. Her particular hate is Catholicism as this religion seems to be an instigator of misery and child abuse; she studied history and read about so much cruelty within the Catholic organisation. She was apposed to the Muslims because of her own sexuality and the way certain Muslim men were vile to her when she was in the spotlight modelling. They considered her to be evil and being a lesbian acting against God by promoting such acts of sexuality. Ruth merely ignored them and continued to live her life in her own way in diffidence of their beliefs, feeling sorry for anyone who had to comply with their beliefs and ignore their own sexual orientation. This made them miserable and some committed suicide as a result of not coping with such a rigid set of rules that restricted their life so much.

THE RIGHT APPROACH

Sharon Green was a student nurse in her second of three years training and was training to be a general nurse but had to gain experience of mental health nursing just as an insight into the area. She had to do 50% theory and 50% practice in her training this was considered a good balance of education and experience, her theory was at a local university and practice in the community and on the wards in a hospital setting. Unfortunately, as good as the education was, nothing prepared them for the cold reality of their practical experience.

They tended to hit the ground running for want of a better expression, the bitter sweet experience soon informed them that things are not always written in stone and the nurse soon learn to think on their feet.

It was fairly quiet on the ward on the day Sharon started; Ruth had a way of instilling a sense of calmness on the ward. The atmosphere was relaxed, the staff had received the verbal handover from the night staff, and they explained about how each patient had been overnight and reported any problems. The night staff appeared tired and keen to go home after what proved to be a busy night, although there were no major incidents to speak of.

Ruth was just waking up having experienced a late night out with her girlfriend and friends, not the usual practice the night before works the next day. But Cheryl's artist friends were up from London and wanted to experience the night life in Manchester. Although Ruth had not been drinking much she was up late and so had to endure the day tired and blinkered, not that she was a morning person anyway. Fortunately, Ruth was working with Alison a young nurse who admired her leadership and skills and tolerated Ruth's lack of self control on these rare occasions. Alison was rather short and slim with short hair and a wicked sense of humour which was appreciated when there was tension on the ward.

Sharon finally arrived for her first day on the ward walking in with a face of dread being brought in by a security guard.

"Another lost soul," he announced.

"Thank you Bill," Ruth said looking at a girl with blonde hair and a blank expression on her face.

Sharon appeared timid and shy, with a look of innocence and slightly apprehensive about starting on the ward as a student nurse. Ruth recognised the look and seemed to empathise as she looked her up and down, frowning at her choice of clothes. The acute mental health units didn't wear uniforms and people just wore ordinary clothes which in this area of the country were called mufti. The idea was to be casual but smart, Sharon had come in with a rather loud T-shirt and jeans, the shirt might as well had said grab me as she had no bra underneath and her breasts were squeezed tightly inside. The only saving grace was her university badge which was pinned above her left breast, saying student nurse Sharon Green.

"You must be Sharon," Ruth said trying to avoid looking at her large breasts.

"Yes," Sharon said shaking her by the hand.

"Come into the office," Ruth said pointing the way.

"Am I in trouble already?" Sharon asked.

"No not really," Ruth replied. "Although you are late and you did miss handover so I need to go through a few things."

"I had trouble with the local transport," Sharon explained.

"Don't worry about that, but do worry about your state of dress, casual dress on here is not T shirt and jeans but a sensible top and trousers otherwise known as mufti!" Ruth explained. "Unless you want to be touched up or spoken to in an inappropriate manner!"

"Understood so shall I go home and get changed?" Sharon asked.

"No just be aware that people may give you strange looks," Ruth said in a professional manner.

Ruth went through a brief handover on the ward and then introduced her to the staff and patients. As predicted patients were looking at Sharon in an admiring manner some of the men were becoming sexually aroused by her appearance made clear by their remarks and the bulge in their trousers.

Ruth hurried Sharon back in the office and sat Sharon down explaining about some of the mental health conditions that she needed to know about. She was introduced to the multi disciplinary team including the occupational therapists, psychologists and psychiatric doctors. Geoff walked in and became fixated on her breasts, having most of his discussion with them and not Sharon's face, which annoyed Sharon and made her feel uncomfortable. Sharon made a point of introducing herself to Geoff before Ruth had chance to say anything which she seemed to do with most of the multi disciplinary team.

"So are you the shrink then?" Sharon asked.

"I am the consultant psychiatrist if that's what you mean," Geoff replied.

"Oh same thing," she said laughing.

"Well I certainly wouldn't consider Geoff a shrink, he is our most respected psychiatrist," Ruth said sharply.

"Quite," Geoff replied embarrassed.

"We have another Ruth here," he said laughing.

"Fuck off Geoff!" Ruth said jokingly.

"Come on she is as you used to be," Geoff said amused. "Now you get a taste of your own medicine!"

"Well they tend to follow methods of practice that went out with the ark, no wonder mental health is falling apart," Sharon said in an opinionated manner.

"My God my girl that is a sweeping statement and I do hope that you have evidence to back your theory," Geoff said abruptly.

"Purely my opinion, but I am sure that I could support what I say with evidence," Sharon said.

"Sharon please kindly refrain from speaking like this to the doctor," Ruth said surprised by her manner.

"Do you want me to keep quiet and not express my opinion?" Sharon said with a surprised look on her face.

"No but I expect you to show respect and wait until you have been here a while before making judgements on the practices of the ward," Ruth said.

"But I am only saying what most students would say or think after all I am a general nurse student on a mental health ward," Sharon said defending herself.

"Oh is that right, crossing the boundaries into another area. You think mental health is sitting people down and sedating them, having a smoking area where patients smoke one cigarette after another or walking round like zombies," Ruth said annoyed.

"Well it seems like that to me," Sharon replied.

"Well may I suggest you observe for yourself and forget all the text book shit until you have been exposed to the real world," Ruth grabbed two of the patient files and dropped them in front of her. "Here read these."

Ruth walked out of the office and down the corridor, leaving Geoff with Sharon

"I think you have upset her," he said waiting for a reaction.

But Sharon sat sulking in the corner of the room and began to read the files.

Ruth stood next to Alison and remained quiet, but Alison sensed her tension.

"How is the student?" Alison asked.

"Don't ask," Ruth replied.

"Is she that bad?" Alison responded.

"Worse, opinionated, rude and annoying," Ruth said.

"Was I that bad as a student?" Alison enquired.

"Not at all you were a model student," Ruth replied. "You were willing to learn and realistic."

"I was also a general nurse who changed to mental health nursing," Alison pointed out.

"I know but she thinks patients are zombies, who smoke and are heavily sedated!" Ruth explained. "It's so fucking frustrating why do we have to keep fighting to defend these people, gone are the days of institutions and asylums, people locked away from the world because they are an embarrassment to society!"

"Look Ruth I am aware of the broken wings and lost souls that you love so much, but unfortunately society hasn't quite caught up yet, yes they are exposed to it on television or in movies or occasionally in the media."

"Oh yes," Ruth butted in. "Schizophrenics who kill people waving samurai swords about saying the voices told them to kill. Voices of command when in reality they of more danger to themselves than others, if they comply with treatment they are fine."

"Like Raven who almost killed you!" Alison said.

"Yes like Raven who was the exception, barking mad!" Ruth said reflecting back.

"Is that a clinical expression?" Alison asked jokingly.

"No but fucking mad is!" Ruth replied laughing.

"A raving lunatic," Alison added. "Deriving from the world Luna meaning moon."

"Definitely true whenever there is a full moon there is trouble on the ward," Ruth said thinking about the worst moments on the ward.

"Do you remember our last full moon when Debbie went mad and tried smashing everything?" Alison reminded Ruth.

"Yes wasn't that something?" Ruth recalled.

"All the poor souls were barking!" Alison agreed.

"A head fuck experience no danger," Ruth said pointing to her head.

"You definitely have a gift for the funicular," Alison said laughing. "Head fuck experience!"

"I guess I am unique!" Ruth admitted.

It was midday and the trolley came up for lunchtime, the regular porter delivered this big trolley full of meals prepared on trays for each patient. Each had their names on from the previous night's food order. The porter looked at Ruth and Alison, he the looked upon Ruth's beautiful face and shapely figure and had to comment.

"Hi gorgeous," he said jovially.

"Hello Paul," Ruth replied echoed by Alison.

"Oh hello Alison," Paul said smiling.

"Oh I see you were referring to Ruth," Alison said jokingly.

"Oh yes although you are nice too," Paul said.

"Too late I am offended now!" Alison said.

"Well I have admired Ruth for a long time," Paul admitted.

"Yes well you know how I feel," Ruth said.

"Yes I know you're a Lesbo!" Paul said disappointed.

"But I can turn you, you would be straight in no time," Paul pleaded.

"Dream on big boy it would take more than you and your prize cucumber to turn me on," Ruth said with a smile.

"Really!" Paul said surprised.

"Yes attractive with nice breasticles and a curvy figure like me," Ruth said prancing round the trolley.

"Oh sorry I have none of the above love," Paul replied.

At that moment Sharon appeared and had obviously been listening to the conversation judging by the expression on her face. She had discovered that Ruth was a lesbian and that was enough for her to hear at this point, she made it obvious that she was homophobic and stood as far away from Ruth as possible as if she had the plague. She waited for Ruth to go away from the trolley and approached Alison.

"So is Ruth gay?" Sharon asked.

"Yes she is a lesbian," Alison said in a matter of fact way. "Why, have you got a problem with that?"

"Not really," Sharon replied obviously lying.

"Well if you have, keep it to yourself okay?" Alison said sternly.

"Fine," Sharon replied with her attitude.

"After all it is her preference and nothing to do with anyone else," Alison insisted.

"It answers questions for me though," Sharon said. "Telling me about my clothes, staring at my breasts like they were on show!"

"Well you are dressed rather tarty if I am honest," Alison remarked.

"So are you a lesbian?" Sharon asked.

"No I am straight, but if I were gay I wouldn't discuss my sex life with a homophobic!" Alison said abruptly.

"I am not homophobic!" Sharon insisted.

"Be honest at least, I can read you like a book, just don't make it obvious to Ruth and don't get upsetting her," Alison warned her.

"God, people are so touchy here," Sharon said sulking.

"I said don't," Alison insisted.

"Okay," Sharon said pulling a face.

"Now help me give out meals," Alison ordered.

Sharon started to give meals out, taking the appropriate trays out to each patient being guided by Alison; she looked very wearily at some of the patients as if they were going to attack her. Sharon had become paranoid about the patients and staff but it was all down to her approach to both, having the right approach was vital to the care of patients and the person centred approach that Carl Rogers talked about in the 1950s was certainly used on the ward. Humanistic nursing was something that was considered popular in the mental health setting with pioneer psychologists such as Abraham Maslow's Hierarchy of needs and Carl Rogers person centred approached practiced daily on the wards. The ward also used nursing models such as Neumann this proved that they did use text book nursing based on theory, but the practical hands on nursing was also important dealing with unpredictable patients like Raven, Colin and others.

But Sharon was not even aware of her own attitude and terminology when getting involved with patients; she was heading for a fall and would not listen to advice from anyone. Ruth could see aspects of herself in Sharon such as not obeying rules, getting involved with patients such as Pamela and certainly not listening to her mentor who was Kathy. But Kathy bailed her out of trouble a number of times and coped with her moods, but Ruth demonstrated her kindness and showed compassion. She also tolerated Sharon because of her own past experience as a student on the ward and her life when she entered the world of modelling. She missed Kathy giving her advice and guiding her back to reality, Kathy was her rock and no mistake. Sharon had studied mental health purely from a text book and never worked on a ward, she was also used to mentors who simply couldn't care less about the students and just filled in the paperwork. Unfortunately, they had no time for students literally due to a busy ward and let the student do what they wanted sometimes unsupervised. Mistakes were made sometimes to the detriment of the patients and students were experiencing bad practice, Ruth didn't want this to happen on her ward and so she insisted on allocated time spent with students.

Ruth tried to explain to Sharon about keeping the noise levels down on the ward anyone disruptive was taken to a low stimuli environment causing less disruption. She explained about using a certain approach none threatening but at the same time showing no fear, she emphasised the need for discretion and limit eye contact. She also explained various psychosis and types of mental illness, such as schizophrenia, bipolar, depression and personality disorders. But Sharon had been talking behind Ruth's back and after a week of receiving reports of Sharon's behaviour Ruth had finally had enough and her patience had ran out.

Ruth called Sharon into the office and asked her to sit down; Sharon had at least begun to wear sensible clothing and looked reasonably smart.

"Look Sharon I need to speak to you about your attitude," Ruth looked angry.

"My attitude?" Sharon said innocently.

"If we lived in an ideal world then we could adopt the same principles as the text book suggests, put it all into practice. But unfortunately we are stuck with reality."

"But changes can be made," Sharon said.

"Yes and we do alter things if we consider what is suggested is practical for this environment," Ruth explained.

"Well research suggests that we adapt to the times and the conditions of the environment," Sharon said cockily.

"For your information patients don't change, the name of their diagnosis may change but they present the same manic depression is now bipolar and multiple personality disorder is dysfunctional identity deficit," Ruth could feel herself boiling up inside.

"Well I think that people are unwilling to change and are stuck in a time zone that restricts them from moving forward," Sharon said smugly.

"Are you suggesting that I am old fashioned?" Ruth asked her.

"Well your methods are quite frankly antiquated," Sharon remarked.

"Well I really can't believe that you have drawn that conclusion after only one week in placement," Ruth stood shocked at Sharon.

"It doesn't take forever to observe old methods and stagnant water has its own odour," Sharon said.

"What a way to describe a clinical environment or mental health unit," Ruth said flabbergasted.

"Well how would you describe this place?" Sharon asked.

"I think you're a very rude young lady and very self opinionated and what's more this is what I think of your text book theories," Ruth said throwing the books across the room and walking out.

Becky heard the end of the conversation and entered the office in a temper

"Never in my career as a nurse have I met anyone so rude," Becky shouted.

"You mean Ruth," Sharon said innocently.

"No I mean you," Becky said pointing at her.

"I was only telling the truth and she threw my books across the room!" Sharon said pointing across the room at the books on the floor.

"No Sharon you were bloody rude and I would have thrown you across the fucking room!" Becky shouted.

"That's nice!" Sharon said sarcastically.

"I shall be writing to your course leader and telling her about your behaviour," Becky threatened.

"I am sorry don't do that," Sharon pleaded.

"My God you have done this before haven't you?" Becky asked. "You have probably left a series of incidents in your past, due to let me see lack of support by your mentor who has been so busy on the ward."

"No time for me that's right," Sharon said.

"Well get a grip and sort your act out we do support you here and you wont get a better mentor than Ruth," Becky tapped her on the shoulder. "So think on. Ruth has been kind to you."

"I know she has she has helped me to learn and understand

things."

"So you should thank her not give her grief!"

"I am grateful believe it or not and I will tell her."

Becky left the office and tried to find Ruth on the ward.

A short while after Sharon decided to find Ruth in order to apologise and thank her for her help. But she noticed a patient called Freda throwing things around the lounge so Sharon intervened. "Now Freda stop it you know that's naughty." Freda spat at Sharon and began pushing and pulling her, she then grabbed Sharon by her hair and swung her around. Sharon tried breaking free and so Freda began to slap her, and then scratched her face and neck.

The incident was witnessed by Ruth and Becky who raced down the corridor to rescue Sharon from Freda, but not before she managed to scratch Sharon's arms. Sharon was escorted to the office by Christine a carer she was shaking and crying, meanwhile Ruth and Becky dealt with Freda. Christine was trying to calm Sharon down but she was inconsolable until Ruth appeared. Oddly enough she put her arms around Ruth and hugged her. "Thank you."

"That's okay," Ruth said looking at Becky in shock.

"I am so sorry for being a pain I will listen from now on." Sharon said sincerely. "I have been a bitch to you; I am going to be a model student from now on."

"I don't expect perfection only one nurse was like that and her name was Kathy," Ruth said winking at Becky.

After this time Ruth was a model student as promised she

spent hours with Ruth and listened intently to all that she said, in fact Sharon would only work with Ruth and when she was off duty so was Sharon. As Ruth said to her she was a student once and a pain in the ass, she would ask all sorts of awkward questions and became attached to Kathy her mentor and best friend.

"Sharon in this life we all have our crosses to bear one of mine was called Colin a real pain in the ass who was a transvestite who dressed like me and killed people, we called him killer queen. Not that I am against transvestites or transsexuals they are okay I have friends like that," Ruth explained.

"And you are a lesbian?" Sharon said confused.

"Yes I am." Ruth admitted.

"But you're so beautiful you could be a model and men must really go for you," Sharon said with surprise.

"Let's not go there," Ruth said smiling. "I was a model once and with a man.

"Wow a model!" Sharon said.

"Yes it's not all it's cracked up to be," Ruth said. "Hard work and too much exposure, TV and travelling."

"This Colin must have been a creep dressing like you and killing people," Sharon said.

"He was the worst creep ever, he actually wanted to be me," Ruth said.

"What happened to him?" Sharon asked.

"He realised he couldn't actually be me and he killed himself, well it was him or me," Ruth explained.

"Were you scared?" Sharon asked.

"Yes I was very scared," Ruth admitted.

Sharon completed her six weeks on the ward and eventually swapped to the mental health course and returned to do her last eight weeks' electives on the ward. She bought chocolates for the ward and a personal porcelain vase for Ruth, oddly enough it resembled the vase her mother had in her lounge, decorated with flowers, and it also had a fine crack in it.

"Cracked porcelain!" Ruth said admiring it.

THE DEMON WITHIN

Survival from abuse is determined by the strength of a person both physically and mentally, the calmness of the individual enables them to think in a logical manner. They rationalise fears and come to terms with them in the best way they know how, but that doesn't mean that they can forget what happened or forgive their abusers. Ruth faced her demons but never forgave them because they were not remorseful, she also had a strange approach to danger due to being attacked and abuse so many times. Her reaction was what else could possibly happen to me that has not already occurred, but she still reacted when somebody touched suddenly or if she smelt certain aftershave it made her sick. You never forget some things they remain hidden in your mind like demons within.

Ruth nursed a man called Julian who appeared quite vulnerable; he presented as effeminate or camp and was picked on at school. He was abducted whilst visiting an unfamiliar city in England at the age of sixteen, he had ran away from home and thought these people were helping him. He had no idea that these people hung around railway stations waiting to pick these people up. Alone and destitute they were easy targets for such monsters to prey on, they moved in like hungry wolves seeking food. They attack with no mercy and conduct their sexual acts of abuse on the vulnerable, leaving them to lick their wounds and that's the lucky ones. Julian did survive but kept the memories in his head every horrible moment and also sounds that would haunt him to his dying day, along with the smells nothing would let him rest. He feared crowds because of male contacts or entering toilets anything that reminded him of his rape, nightmares occurred every time he slept, these were his demons within. Ruth tried to comfort him when he awoke screaming or hitting cupboards or walls with his fists. She felt his pain and wanted to unburden him with his demons, all due to the acts of abuse that they both suffered. No one knows this world but those abused, no one can feel the pain like they do, they are never free to walk in public places or feel comfortable anywhere but home. If you see a person looking apprehensive at a railway station or another public place or squeezing through a crowd nervously, they could have been abused. Like a person who enters a male toilet and rushes into a cubical in order to avoid other people, clutching their luggage and holding it close to their body for protection.

Julian attempted to committing suicide when he felt that he couldn't cope with the demons inside as they took over his mind and made him miserable. He tried pills and even tried jumping off a railway bridge; he was stopped by the police a passing patrol car caught him as he climbed up to jump off a wall. A police woman persuaded him to come down and he fell to the ground lying in a foetal position crying. She put her arms around him as if he were an infant in distress; he soon calmed down and spoke about his past as if he had known Ruth forever.

Ruth seemed like a big sister to him the kind that he could look up to and respect, Ruth was disgusted by the way he was treated at school, college and in the work place. Julian had a number of issues relating to his rape and like Ruth he had to address them, Ruth suggested counselling with the right person to relate to building a therapeutic relationship with her. She advised a female due to his circumstances, a male would cause further problems and exacerbate his situation even further.

Julian progressed thanks to Ruth and began to adjust to the environment with minimal problems, his nightmares would probably still happen as he slept each night but he could deal with that, he could also face the demons in his head. Ruth still had the occasional nightmare and panic attack, but she learned how to deal with this and being part of society as a square peg in a round hole as she described it. Julian began working in a clothes shop around women of various ages they accepted Julian for what he was and he really enjoyed his work. Ruth was pleased that Julian was considered a success story despite his traumatic history, most youths going through this would have committed suicide. Ruth was pleased to be able to help Julian and watch his progress over the months until he was settled and comfortable. The sad part is that his attackers got away with what they did, they live to victimise and rape others they are known as monsters. But one day they will answer for their crimes, justice is always around the corner and these people need to be caught for the safety of others in order to prevent any more acts of abuse.

MONSTER

The ward was fairly quiet except for a few patients having outbursts and one running up and down the corridors. But it was certainly nothing that the staff couldn't handle, especially with Ruth in charge and Rebecca at her side. Alison was busy trying to calm down the patients, Ruth spoke to a patient called Mary who was bipolar she was the one running up and down the ward in her manic state.

Ruth had enjoyed her weekend with Cheryl; they had spent time with a few transvestite friends in Manchester's gay bars down Canal Street. One of them was called John but when they were out at night he became she and called Jennifer a slim lady with long dark hair and dressed so elegantly. Doris was a little older and less attractive as a woman but he or she didn't care. Ruth discussed her weekend with Rebecca and Alison who promised to go out with them one day, Sheena and Gloria like to go occasionally and they are heterosexuals. Ruth was so excited about her weekend out that she was unprepared for the new admission and certainly not expecting a challenge.

Graham Layton was a thirty-year-old man from Denton and was admitted under police protection as a paedophile claiming to be suffering from depression. He claimed it was long term depression and as he had mental health problems he would be admitted onto the ward and therefore protected from harm. The police were convinced that he was avoiding imprisonment for the crime of abusing children and those prisoners would most certainly harm him. The question was who was going to interview such a man and find out more about his questionable mental illness.

Ruth decided that she was the only one who hadn't got children and despite her own history of abuse she needed to prove that she had the strength to interview him despite the fact that his features were like Malcolm and acted like Ron her own abuser.

"Are you sure that you want to interview Graham?" Rebecca asked.

"Yes I do," Ruth replied.

"We will be close by if you need us Ruth," Alison said concerned.

"Thank you ladies I will be fine," Ruth replied bravely.

Ruth began by taking deep breaths and then picking up a pen and paper, she was trying to clear her mind of all thoughts, making sure that her mind wasn't clouded by anything. She needed to focus on the situation and not let anything influence her judgement of the patient, her job was to be non judgmental and simply write down the facts as Graham presented them.

"Ruth, are you sure you're okay?" Rebecca asked.

"Becky, please I need to do this," Ruth insisted.

"Okay Ruth," Rebecca said reluctantly.

Ruth smiled confidently and left the office, she walked slowly across the corridor to the interview room where

Graham sat calmly in an easy chair. Ruth glanced across at her colleagues and then sat opposite Graham in view of the office and near the panic button by the door. She remembered Raven when she attacked her in that very room and she was unable to reach the button. Graham was a fat man with short cropped hair and glasses with thick lenses; he wore a scruffy shirt and baggy trousers. Ruth could smell a mixture of body sweat and cheap after shave much like the type Ron wore her stomach began to churn and her mouth was wet as if she was going to be sick. But Ruth was determined to interview him and so endured the horrible smells and his horrid looks in order to obtain the information she needed. She tried to avoid eye contact but she felt if she looked at him it might stop her smelling him.

"I am Ruth and I will be interviewing you today," Ruth said.

"I am Graham," he held out his hand in friendship.

Ruth declined and instead held her pen and paper up. "Do you mind me writing things down?" she asked politely.

"We may have a problem here," Rebecca said. "Ruth seems uneasy"

"You know what she said, she wouldn't appreciate us butting in," Alison said.

Graham sensed Ruth's feelings towards him and deliberately began to antagonise her. Ruth felt uneasy and very uncomfortable but continued her interview trying to write but just fidgeting with the pen.

"I have been depressed for years I had a rough childhood, my parents were strict and we were never close. They stopped me playing with dolls and make up; you know the type of things I mean." He said trying to make eye contact.

"I have your basic details such as your age, date of birth and last address," Ruth said.

"I don't live there now as my neighbours persecuted me and threatened to kill me because I stood by their children's school, I have bruises from where they punched and kicked me." He stood up and went to remove his shirt. "Do you want to see?"

Rebecca stood up about to leave the office, but Alison stopped her.

"Its okay, he is sitting back down," Alison said reassuring Rebecca.

"Sit down Graham I don't need to see that," Ruth said.

"You don't like me do you?" he asked Ruth.

"My opinion is irrelevant; I am a professional mental health nurse doing my job."

"Then I will tell you about me," Graham continued.

"I have felt low in mood lately and had suicidal thoughts, but I have never attempted suicide, I don't want to be like I am with children but I can't help it. These thoughts are in my head and I can't get them out, I have tried and gone to specialists but they don't help me not really."

"So are you saying it is right to abuse children, are you actually telling me that," Ruth said nervously.

"Yes I am driven with desire as if I am instructed by God,"

Graham appeared to believe what he was saying in a strange and twisted way.

"You mention God as if you truly believe in God," Ruth said trying to understand him. "What religion are you?"

"Catholic I go to confession." he said.

"You are Roman catholic?" Ruth asked. "And you go to confession for forgiveness," Ruth looked across at Rebecca and Alison then back at him.

"You seem surprised" he said. "Are you?"

"Not at all," Ruth said thinking about her arguments with the priests.

"I pleaded with God to help me and set me free," he said.

Ruth bit her lip hard and began writing, she could feel pain from her lip and touched it with her hand, when she looked she noticed blood on her hand.

"I need help and protection can you guarantee this for me?" he pleaded.

"We assess the situation, make notes and the doctor makes the ultimate decision based on the facts presented from observations and the things you say. Only the doctor can determine whether or not you are mentally ill and able to stay here," Ruth said reluctantly.

"Well I put myself in your good and capable hands," he said smiling.

Ruth was starting to feel sick again and her mind was beginning to wander into past traumas and her childhood abuse. She could also see Malcolm sitting opposite and she suddenly stood up and excusing herself

"That's our queue to rescue her," Rebecca said rushing out of the office with Alison close behind her. "Let's get her out of there."

"But how are we going to do this?" Alison said.

"Leave it to me, stand by," Rebecca said. "Ruth I need you urgently," Rebecca shouted.

Ruth headed for the door. "Coming Becky's" She turned back and addressed Graham. "See you later."

Ruth entered the office in a state, shaking and a bleeding lip.

"Christ Ruth you really didn't need to interview that creep," Rebecca said.

"He's a monster," Ruth said. "But I had to do it for my own sake."

"Well you did well," Rebecca said patting her on the back.

Ruth suddenly jumped and ran to the staff toilet and began being sick, she held her stomach and vomited in the bowel. Alison followed her in and stood rubbing her back.

"Ruth are you okay?" Alison asked.

"Yes I will be," Ruth said grabbing a piece of toilet roll.

"Shit Ruth you did a really brave thing out there; I would have slapped the fucker!" Alison admitted. "God I am so proud of you."

"I did my job that's all," Ruth said trying to stop her eyes from watering.

"He is such a slime ball I hate him," Alison said angrily.

"Alison," Ruth said coming out of the cubical. "You have to be professional really." Ruth started washing her face. "Whether you like it or not."

"Well he's a real monster and I think of my children and what he could do to them," she said concerned. "We should not be protecting the likes of him."

"Alison please I have more reason than most for hating monsters like him, but as a nurse I have to help him," Ruth said calmly.

"It must have been so hard for you to interview him, while Rebecca and I looked on," Alison said concerned.

"Look Alison, don't get me wrong I would like to castrate that fucker but I can't and you know what really hurts is that the system protects them. They live in our community and we don't know where, they stand outside schools and snatch kids. They befriend families and abuse their children, is that right or fair fuck no, that's the shit system with live in, so fucking deal with it!" Ruth shouted angrily.

"It's fucking shit!" Ruth said hitting her fists on the sink.

"Ruth please we all have anger and tears for those who suffer," Alison opened her arms to hug her and Ruth cried on her shoulder Alison cried too.

Later that day Ruth was in the office with Rebecca writing notes.

"You know he's not mentally ill don't you?" Rebecca said.

"Of course I do; why do you say that?" Ruth asked.

"Because I know you and the good that you see in everyone," Rebecca said.

"Not in that monster," Ruth replied.

"Then we need to prove it," Rebecca said.

"I know, but bastards like him are clever," Ruth said concerned.

"Oh don't worry people like him trip themselves up," Rebecca said tapping her head with her finger. "Alison and I will be watching him you just keep your distance."

"What will that achieve Becky, he is so cunning, he will slither away like a snake," Ruth did the motions of a snake with her arm.

"Trust me I have dealt with his sort before," Rebecca said confidently.

"Good luck with that one!" Ruth said smiling.

The days passed with little activity Ruth was off duty and Rebecca was watching Graham, Alison was also observing him at times. However, it wasn't until Ruth returned that Graham decided to misbehave and follow Ruth around, she was aware of his presence having been followed many times before by Malcolm and Colin mainly. But what did he want from Ruth, he was confident that he was getting what he wanted by pretending to be mentally ill. So did he expect more than this or did he get pleasure out of just following her and making her nervous, was this a power game for him, a way of seeing pleasure from watching people suffer? He had obviously sensed her fear and was drawn to it like a lion to meat, it was like a craving that wouldn't go away and once again Ruth was the victim.

Alison was close by watching him and making mental notes of his behaviour, she wanted to tell him to stop but she needed evidence to prove that he was sane. Geoff was in the office looking very content and looking through Graham's paperwork. Ruth entered the office looking distraught and pacing back and forth.

"Okay what the fucks going on?" Ruth shouted.

"What do you mean?" Geoff said bewildered.

"That monster Graham is he stopping?" Ruth asked.

"No not at all," Geoff replied surprised by her behaviour.

"Well he just said he has won," Ruth explained. "So he's won what exactly?"

"He's winding you up trying to get a reaction, you're his toy," Geoff said. "Anyway you usually fight for the patients; I haven't seen you like this for a long time, what's wrong?" Geoff seemed concerned.

"He's a fucking monster, a paedophile, he doesn't belong here," Ruth said shaking.

"So prove it!" Geoff said.

"What?" Ruth couldn't believe what she had heard.

"Oh I agree with you so stop being so anal and prove it,"

Geoff was trying in his own way to calm her down.

"And, how the fuck do I do that Geoff?" Ruth said looking out of the office window at Graham sitting on a seat. "Look at him watching me and thinking I actually like him!"

"I can," Alison said entering the office. "He has just been talking to another patient bragging how he managed to fool Ruth and get his own way, he said Ruth will protect him and speak up for him to the police, and he also said that you promised to help him!"

"It's all lies you don't believe him do you?" Ruth asked.

"No of course not he is lying, he's a devious prick," Alison said.

"Right let's play him at his own game," Geoff said. "We too can be cunning and devious!"

A few more days passed, Graham was acting rationally Ruth stayed out of the way and allowed Rebecca and Alison to watch him. He was talking to patients and at one stage asked to tidy his bed and clean his own room as a form of therapy. Unaware that he was being monitored and manoeuvred in to proving that he was not depressed he did exactly as requested. He was invited to join in activities and even assist others in getting involved with board games and arts crafts. In doctors ward round he appeared confident and had a positive outlook. There was no evidence of depression, but he continued to brag to patients about pulling the wool over Ruth's eyes and how gullible she was, he even laughed at the thought of terrorising her due to her vulnerable state.

The next day Ruth, Rebecca and Alison joined Geoff to

discuss Graham's progress.

"Well Ruth you look better today," Geoff said smiling.

"Yes thank you," Ruth said smiling back.

"So about Graham what's the verdict?" Geoff asked.

"Ask them," Ruth insisted.

"I am asking you as the senior nurse, you tell me," Geoff said watching her reaction.

"Graham is a monster!" Ruth replied.

"No professionally, I can't tell the police that!" Geoff said.

"Okay," Ruth took a deep breath and began. "Graham showed no signs or symptoms of having depression; he appeared positive and was involved with many activities with the occupational therapists. He assisted with activities with other patients and kept his own room clean and tidy which if he was depressed he would struggle to act in this way. At no time did he express any negative thoughts or suggest thoughts of suicide, he acted rationally at all times throughout his stay on the ward."

"Do you ladies agree?" Geoff asked.

"Absolutely," Rebecca said in agreement.

"No doubt in my mind," Alison said.

"Then I will arrange his discharge from here and contact the police as soon as possible," Geoff said.

"He has confessed to many cases of abuse and we are all willing to make statements accordingly," Ruth said.

"So let's send him to hell!" Alison said.

Later that afternoon the police arrived and arrested Graham, they walked past the staff and Graham struggled as he passed Ruth, she had her back to him.

Graham looked back at her.

"You promised to help me, now you are turning your back on me," he shouted.

Ruth turned to face him with anger in her eyes. "Don't even go there," Ruth shouted. "You betrayed yourself by your behaviour and blame me for that, don't you dare put the blame on me!"

"I told you that I was depressed," he continued. "I am mentally ill."

"No you are a monster and God help you when you go to prison, the prisoners will tear you apart."

Rebecca grabbed Ruth's arm. "Yes you are right Ruth he will be sorry," Becky shouted.

"Take that scum away," Alison shouted.

Graham was escorted out of the building and into a van and he was never seen at the hospital again.

"We were so unprofessional then," Ruth said.

"Do I look like I actually care," Rebecca grinning.

"Tell me Becky was he right to blame me?" Ruth asked.

"Are you serious?" Becky said astonished by Ruth's question. "Honestly sometimes Ruth you amaze me with your intellectual mind!" she said sarcastically. "Yes you are to blame for protecting the children from monsters like him!"

"Yes you're right he is to blame not us," Ruth agreed.

"Yes Ruth don't you ever blame yourself," Alison said. "Ruth you just love everyone and blame yourself when mistakes are made, but he deserved what he got!"

"Let's go out tonight and have a few well-earned drinks," Rebecca said.

"Sounds good to me," Ruth agreed.

"Count me in," Alison said.

I must point out that the events in this are true and that justice was served in this case. The characters were also real but obviously had different names and their true identities kept secret due to confidentiality. It should be noted that not all paedophiles are caught and some roam amongst us in society, causing harm to children these should be stopped. Some of them are also released from prison and put children at risk, they are given accommodation and no one knows where they are as this information is also confidential. This is obviously a fault within the justice system and other people are to blame for this, but how do they sleep at night knowing that they are partly responsible for ruining children's lives. Ruth spent her life being haunted by her past and experiencing night terrors due to her abuse, who thinks of the victims when they are accommodating and helping paedophiles back into society. Unless you are a victim like Ruth you will never fully understand the pain and anxiety that lives with your years after the incidents. The victims need to group together and take action in order to prevent others suffering, help to keep these monsters off the streets and put somewhere where they can cause no harm.

Ruth managed to deal with her demons and with help from friends did adjust and lived with minimum anxiety in her life, she used coping strategies such as detersive thought therapy and counselling. She also campaigned against letting these monsters on the street by holding demonstrations and publicly discussing her own experiences along with other victims on television and in newspaper articles. Ruth was a happier person feeling that she had contributed in bringing about changes in society; she was determined to carry on this fight until something was done to make society a safer place for vulnerable people, particularly women and children who were suffering from abuse. Ruth never wanted to be put on a pedestal and didn't seek fame or glory, but she as a victim had to come forward and lead the fight against abuse. Ruth is known as a brave and caring woman who is loved by her friends and colleagues, she continues to be popular wherever she goes and she is considered by many as the girl next door with her innocent looking eyes and her warm winning smile. She helped such people as Fiona from Criminal World magazine providing answers to crimes, her knowledge of mental health proved most useful in solving cases. Such as in the case of the Harrington curse and the curse of Zyanya, she became part of the crime solving team on many occasions. She enjoyed helping them and continues to offer her services to them whenever she is needed, in fact she was invited on a cruise in order to investigate missing persons aboard a ship, but that's another story!

SRS BOOKS

CRACKED PORCELAIN FULL STORY

CRACKED PORCELAIN FULL STORY TWO -BROKEN WINGS AND LOST SOULS

CRACKED PORCELAIN FULL STORY THREE- REMEMBER ME

CONFLICT OF FAITH

STORIES BEYOND BELIEF

DOUBLE EXPOSURE

ULTIMATE PURPOSE

OPERATION BRAINSTORM

FOR THE LOVE OF CHARLOTTE

THE HARRINGTON CURSE

CURSE OF ZYANYA

THE ADVENTURES OF THE TIME WITCHES

EIGHT SKULLS OF TEVERSHAM

CURSED
USEFUL ADDRESSES

RACE FOR LIFE
http://raceforlife.cancerresearchuk.org/index.html

MANCHESTER PRIDE
http://www.manchesterpride.com

INTERNATIONAL GAY PRIDE
http://www.nighttours.com/gaypride

NEW YORK
https://www.nycpride.org

ABUSE
http://thisisabuse.direct.gov.uk

ABUSE U.S.A
https://www.childhelp.org/hotline

GENDER EQUALITY
http://www.equalityhumanrights.com/about-us/about-commission/our-vision-and-mission/our-business-plan/gender-equality

DOMESTIC VIOLENCE
http://www.helpguide.org/articles/abuse/domestic-violence-and-abuse

BOOK CLUBS IN MANCHESTER
http://bookclub.meetup.com/cities/gb/18/manchester

INTERNATIONAL BOOK CLUBS
http://www.readerscircle.org

WHY BOOK CLUBS?
http://www.slate.com/articles/news_and_politics/assessment/2011/07/book_clubs.html